A
STRANGE
CODE
OF
JUSTICE

A Black Bat Mystery

Reymoure Keith Isely

A
STRANGE
CODE
OF
JUSTICE

The Bobbs-Merrill Company, Inc.
Indianapolis/New York

ISBN 0-672-51935-6
Library of Congress catalog card number 73-22659
Designed by Sheila Lynch
Manufactured in the United States of America

First printing

Bill Ellwood and Stan Seay—for assistance

A
STRANGE
CODE
OF
JUSTICE

How long soever it hath continued,
if it be against reason,
it is of no force in law.

Sir Edward Coke

THURSDAY

1

It was pitch black out there.

Any moon there might have been was smothered in the blackness of the storm. The wind found the break in the mountains and roared through, driving the rain against the back of his neck like pellets of ice as he hunkered there, splattering it against the window in front of him with the relentless monotony of a thousand small drums. And the drops welded together, forming rivulets and trickles that ran down the glass, making everything in the room appear wavy and distorted and hard for him to see. But he could see. He brushed the glass with his hand, and he could see there through that space right under the blind.

They were doing it!

The bedlight was on and he could see them. They were. He was right there on top of her and they were doing it. She was digging her feet into the bed and lifting him high, and he knew what was happening now. Her mouth was moving and he knew what she was saying. Faster, faster, higher, higher.

Then everything became blurry. Maybe it was the rain. But maybe it was something else, a terrible blindness of rage. He pushed himself away from the house, leaped to his feet and raced to the door.

He was prepared to break through the door. But, strangely, the door stood open. He charged into the darkened room and straight for the dim light of the bedroom. The floor was bedded

deep in soft carpet. Maybe it was this. Perhaps it was the preoc-
cupation of their ecstasies. Anyway, they didn't hear him coming. Her eyes were closed and she didn't see him bound around
the end of the bed, didn't realize at all what was happening
when he grabbed him by the back of the hair and jerked him
free of her. She uttered a breathless exclamation of delight.
Then she opened her eyes in puzzlement, and the puzzlement
was instantly displaced by terror. She opened her mouth to
scream. But she did not scream.

He had him by the throat now and the man fought back.
Then something seemed to snap in his neck and he no longer
fought back, and his body became heavy in his hands. So he
opened his hands and the other fell to the floor, this seducer of
women.

"Did you kill him?" she asked.

He did not know. He did not care. And he did not answer.

He looked at her. She was still naked, standing there against
the wall. Her skin looked all sweaty and the hair at her crotch
was all gooey and ugly with what she had been doing.

"Are you going to kill me, too?" she asked. But there was no
real fear in her voice.

He looked at her. He began to cry.

2

Lightning exploded.

For a flashing instant all motion seemed to cease. The mountains were statically cast in a brittle, eerie light as from an
enormous blue flashbulb.

Then darkness.

The car left the road. The front wheels hung in space. For an
agonizing moment the headlights shone straight ahead like

small, futile beacons, losing themselves in a vast arena of infinite blackness. Then they began to arc downward.

The car disappeared. Wood smashed. Metal rended. The headlights went out.

The rain continued to fall gently in the mountains.

FRIDAY

1

Titan—snuggled in the mountains—was beautiful in the midmorning sun. Oak Street with its magnificent trees, wet leaves glistening, could boast as much beauty as any.

Sam Powell drove his cruiser leisurely along the street, drew to a stop in front of a large white frame house and got out. He wore a Stetson-style deputy's hat. But the rest of his uniform was hidden away someplace in his closet back at the boarding house. He seldom dressed in full uniform, and nobody had ever insisted that he should. In its place he wore a light jacket and a pair of dark green serge trousers. His boots were black, large and comfortable.

Sam was a comfortable-looking man with a quiet, casual manner. He stood under six feet, but his shoulders and chest were massive, his hands large and powerful, with thick heavy-duty wrists. Solid as a rock. He was close to thirty-five, but the broad square-jawed face made him look older. The soft gray eyes possessed a lazy twinkle that complimented the casual manner. But the mouth contradicted it. There was a stubborn, aggressive cut to the mouth that told the true story.

He studied the large white house almost reminiscently, then walked around behind where Aida Marshal was tending her garden. She was sixty-five years old. Through the years Sam had come to look upon her almost as a mother.

"Nice to see you, Sam. It's been a while."

Sam nodded.

"Too long a while, Sam." She offered him a chair, then, "I'll get right to the point. I hear things are not going too smoothly between you and Justine. I'm asking you to be patient with her, Sam. She's made a mistake, she knows it and she's just putting up a bitter hard front. You can't be too hard on her, Sam."

"I understand," he said.

"Then you won't walk out on her?"

You couldn't read much from Sam's face.

"Sam," she asked again, "you're not planning to walk out on her?"

"No."

Aida sighed a breath of relief. "The people in this county think highly of you. The only reason they elected Justine as sheriff was because she was Sandy Marshal's daughter. And the only reason she ran for the office was because she thought Sandy would have expected it.

"It's a tradition here in Titan to have a Marshal in the sheriff's office. The people felt they could kill two birds at once. They could elect Justine and still have you to stay on and run things just as you did during that year of my husband's illness."

"Justine and I used to be pretty good friends," Sam said. "We'll work it out."

"Hearing you say that makes me feel a good deal younger. Can I rest my mind, then, that you've turned down that offer?"

"What offer?"

"Now, now, Sam. Isn't it true that you received an attractive offer as some kind of an investigator in Washington?"

Sam grinned. "I received it. And I turned it down."

Her faded eyes were steeped in wisdom. "Wasn't it, perhaps, suggested to you that you could take the investigative job temporarily and then return in time for the next election and run again for sheriff?"

"It was."

"That's a pretty enticing offer to turn down. Why?"

He shrugged.

"Was it," she asked, "—was it because you thought it was a setup?"

He did not reply.

"Well *I* think it was a setup," she said. "And so do you. You know every bit as well as I do that ever since they put in that big highway through the mountains there have been strong forces at work downtown to have Titan County fall under the jurisdiction of the state police. That would virtually destroy the sheriff's office.

"And *you* don't think Justine would be a match for those people downtown. And," she added crisply, "you're right! She's smart as a whip, mind you. And she's nobody's fool. But she is *not* Sandy Marshal."

"Aida?" Sam said.

"Yes?"

"I'm not Sandy Marshal either."

She accepted that, nodded. "No . . . you've never tried to be anything but what you are. And Sandy told me more than once that Sam Powell was the smartest—if you'll pardon the expression coming from an old lady—the smartest 'son of a bitch' deputy he ever worked with."

Sam grinned; then his broad shoulders began shaking as he laughed softly to himself. "So Sandy called me a son of a bitch, did he?"

"Many times," she said, smiling. "Many times."

Frieda Munsterburg, Aida's hired girl, brought them coffee in the garden.

"Wilbur! Wilbur!" a voice cried.

There was a note of alarm in that voice. Gertie Hancock, Aida's sister, stood on the back step of the house next door. She walked down the steps and headed toward the garage at the rear.

"Good *morning,* Gertie," Aida called.

But Gertie did not hear her and was soon hidden by the thick hedges separating the two yards.

"I see your sister is in visiting Wilbur," Sam observed.

"I'm afraid it's more than a visit," Aida replied glumly. "I think Barbara has run out on Wilbur and little Bobby. Neither Gertie nor Wilbur has said anything, but Justine picked up Barbara on the street yesterday and drove her to the bus depot. Justine said Barbara was carrying her luggage. . . . I suppose it had to happen sooner or later. She was no good for him, Sam. She was . . ."

Sam nodded. He knew all about Barbara Hancock.

"It isn't the first time she's walked out on him," Aida said. "But somehow I think this time—"

The morning air was ripped open by a loud, piercing, terrified scream. The surrounding buildings reechoed the sound until it was difficult to know from which direction it had come.

But Sam knew.

He burst through the hedge, raced across Wilbur's garden toward the garage. The side door of the garage stood open. He immediately noticed the pair of women's shoes protruding, toes downward, from the open doorway. Gertie Hancock. She was lying motionless with her head face-down on the concrete floor.

A short distance away, sprawled on the floor beside the car, was Wilbur.

The main door of the garage was closed. The engine of the car was idling. Sam bounded to the car and turned off the ignition. Wilbur weighed more than 200 pounds, but Sam lifted him bodily, carried him outside, and laid him on the ground.

Wilbur's forehead was skinned. Also—Sam took a closer look. In addition to the skinned forehead, four deep, narrow scratches extended from his left cheekbone, down his cheek and along the full length of his neck to the shirt collar—as if his face had been raked by someone's fingernails. And, whereas the injury to the forehead appeared fresh, those fingernail scratches on his cheek had already begun to form scabs.

He was still breathing.

Sam strode over to Gertie, rolled her onto her back. He nose had been flattened by her fall and appeared to be broken. Her cheeks and lips were covered with blood and mucus. Her breathing was irregular and labored.

Aida stood at his side now, staring down at her sister. "She's had a heart attack, Sam. Phone the hospital and have them prepared."

He made the call, then stood beside the phone a moment rubbing the side of his nose thoughtfully. Wilbur was looked upon by many as being somewhat simple and insensitive. Yet there wasn't a doubt in the world he had deliberately attempted suicide.

SATURDAY

1

10:20 P.M.

Sam Powell left Homer Buchanan's office in the large Lakeside Hotel, nodded to the desk clerk and went directly upstairs. He stopped at suite 22 and knocked.

There was an indication of sound but no immediate answer. He knocked again.

"Who's it?" A woman's voice. Young. Slightly thick.

"Sam Powell."

"So? Who the hell is Sam Pow——?" The voice stopped as if muffled.

Sam could detect the faint sibilance of whispering. He waited, then knocked again.

"Hold on. Wait'll I get something on." The door opened and a dark-complexioned girl, thick hair askew, showed her face. "Yeah? . . . Yes?" She breathed liquor.

Sam placed a large hand against the panel of the door and slowly but firmly pushed it open. The girl was forced to give ground. He entered the room and closed the door.

She was young enough. Twenty, maybe a bit more. But her eyes weren't that young. In the right mood she could have been a pretty girl. She wore a heavy perfume infringed upon by musk and liquor fumes. She had thrown a terrycloth kimono over her shoulders but was naked underneath. The terrycloth wasn't concealing many of her properties. But she was more hostile

11

than embarrassed. And just a teeny bit frightened, maybe . . .

"You can't come barging—"

"Where's Pepe?" He looked around the room. The Lakeside
was the oldest hotel in town and still, in a lot of people's estima-
tion, the most prestigious. Suite 22 was way out of Pepe Poirier's
class.

"I've got no reason to hide." Pepe sauntered in from an adjoining room wearing a padded jockstrap and a pair of white
shoes. He was thin, about five-seven; thick black hair stood out
prominently against his prison pallor. "What's the sweat, Sam?"

"You've got Homer worried. When he found your name on
his register he damned near crapped himself."

Pepe smiled. A good smile, square and gleeful. "I can see his
face." Pepe chortled. This was his type of humor.

Sam grinned. Despite the fact that Pepe's sense of values was
distorted and in some ways virtually rotten, Sam had always
been susceptible to his humor. To Pepe life was a game. Win or
lose, he apparently held no rancor. Sam had sent him to prison
once, eight years ago. For the past seven years they had had an
agreement. Eventually Pepe would break that agreement. In
the meantime Titan was the better for it.

Sam said, "Homer's scared silly your little friend here is going
to use this suite as her working headquarters."

"Them words hurt, Sam. That's a terrible thing to say about
my wife."

Sam remained silent. Pepe was a compulsive talker.

"Now, Sam, you know I wouldn't move over here into the
high part of town and try a thing like that. It'd cause trouble.
You and I got an agreement. For six, seven years now. I don't
cause you trouble I can live here in Titan. I like that agreement,
Sam. I like Titan. I want to cause trouble I go somewheres else.
I don't break the agreement, Sam."

Sam caught motion in the corner of his eye. A mirror on
the wall to his right had reflected the movements of the girl.

She had doffed her kimono, was trying to step into a pair of black panties, and was making a bad job of it. She was drunk.

Pepe also was drunk. But he could hold his liquor.

"You've got me worried, Pepe."

"No trouble from me, Sam. A promise."

"When I see you celebrate like this? I've got to worry."

"I just spent twenty-two months up there behind the wall. Ain't I got a right to celebrate?"

"This suite comes high. You paid a week's advance. That's a lot of money. Where did it come from?"

"I hit Vegas before I came here. I was lucky. Jesus, I made—" Sam shook his head.

"I'm lying to you, Sam? You saying that?"

"You didn't have money five days ago when you got into town."

"That ain't so."

"The day you hit town you took your woman to Doc Blainsworth and got a health clearance. You were shacked in down at Solly Miner's motel. Your girl here was hooking at five bucks and she started the day you hit town. Hell, Pepe, you didn't even have enough money to give Solly a down payment on the room."

Pepe licked his lips nervously.

"And," Sam said, "I know within twenty bucks how much your woman made for you, and it isn't enough to afford this place. Let's see your wallet."

"Ain't I got no rights?"

"You're fast using them up. The wallet."

"Sure."

He led Sam into the adjoining room. A bedroom. A pair of trousers was piled at the foot of the unmade bed. He drew out a wallet from the hip pocket and handed it to Sam.

"All I want is to feel like a citizen, Sam. For a few days . . ."

There was a driver's license, social security card, an ace of spades and twenty-five dollars.

"Do you own a car?"

"No."

"This *all* your money?"

There was a noticeable hesitation. "Yeh."

"How about the girl?"

"I handle the money. She might have two, three dollars. Nothing more."

Sam returned the wallet. "Put on your clothes. I'm taking you in."

"I don't get it. What's wrong?"

"I'm going to stop the trouble before it begins. You should have had sense enough to stay over at Solly's where you belong."

"Sam?"

"It's pretty clear what you've got in mind. You checked out of Solly's. You checked in here, paid seven days' advance. All you've got left is twenty-five dollars. Are you figuring to buy enough booze and food for seven days on that? Put on your clothes."

Pepe licked his lips, looked up at Sam, lowered his eyes. "What's the charge going to be?"

"Procuring. Subsection one, either h or j. I haven't decided yet."

"You going to *frame* me, Sam?"

"Put on your clothes."

"You can't take me on procuring. I'm clean. There's been nobody in this room but Delores and me. Honest to Christ!"

"There were plenty in your room at Solly's."

"You gonna take me on *that?*"

"Right."

"But we got a *deal!*"

"The sheriff's office doesn't make deals."

Which wasn't completely true. Prostitution was one of the realities you had to live with in a place like Titan, what with the massive coal mines to the south, the lumber operations to the west and north, and the large tourist trade. Sandy Marshal had learned this the hard way almost thirty years ago when he had swept the valley clean of a large, well-organized prostitution ring. The vacuum had been filled by an influx of degenerate sluts from all over the country, and the result had been disease and chaos. And so prostitution—controlled prostitution—was one of those necessary evils.

Although Sam had never literally made a *deal* with Pepe, he had let the ex-convict understand, years ago, that if he had a woman that was certified disease-free, if he kept his operations down in that part of town where they belonged, if he didn't attempt any bunco and stayed out of trouble, then the sheriff's office wouldn't go out of its way to cause him trouble.

This had a twofold effect. It gave Sam a hold over Pepe which he could apply at any given moment. And it kept Pepe in spending money, so that, at least while he was in Titan, he was not plying his trade as a thief.

Pepe was very pale. "They'll crucify me, Sam. With my record they'll crucify me."

Sam said nothing.

"But what about our *agreement?*"

"If we had any kind of an agreement," Sam said, "you broke it when you moved over here to set up business. You're through in Titan."

Pepe was stone sober. And he was scared. He seemed about to say something. Sam waited. But Pepe changed his mind and reached for his trousers.

"Hand me that cup out of your jockstrap." Sam checked the stitching, felt the padding, then returned it.

Pepe sat on the edge of the bed. It rocked slightly. Sam studied it thoughtfully, took a step toward it when he heard a door open in the other room.

He ran from the bedroom in time to see the girl disappear into the hall. He returned to the bedroom, picked up the phone and got the desk clerk.

"Sam Powell. Poirier's woman is running away. Stop her and hold her. I'll be down in a minute. Watch it. She could be tough."

"Don't worry."

Sam motioned to Pepe and allowed the ex-convict to walk in front of him. He removed the key from the door and locked it as they left.

Downstairs by the entrance the desk clerk was lying on his side, holding his stomach, knees doubled, writhing. His breath came in stertorous gasps through his open mouth. ". . . kicked . . . ungg . . . balls . . ."

Sam ran to the street as a car roared away from the curb. He couldn't make out the model, and the vapor streetlights made it impossible to determine the true color.

He picked up the desk clerk and gently laid him on a lounge in the lobby.

He started toward the switchboard. "Okay, Pepe. What's your car? And the license number."

"I told you. I don't own a car."

"Well, what car is she driving?"

"I didn't see. I was in here, Sam."

Sam waited a moment, then walked behind the desk and dialed a number.

"Sheriff's office." That was Phil Silvers.

"Phil. Sam. You were taking a count on Pepe Poirier's motel room day before yesterday. What was he using for a car?"

"Sure. Got it in the file. Hold on . . . a '69 Corvette, two-door, light blue, Utah license 126.4839. Serial—"

"Never mind that right now. Who owns the car?"

"The girl. Delores Mink."

"Ming?"

"Mink."

"Mink?"

"From Indian blood. Changed it from Mingoose. So they say."

"She's not from the valley."

"No. Poirier brought her in."

"She's lit out. Chances are she'll try and leave town."

"I'm free. Want me to pick her up? I can get Lena to run the board."

"No. We'd better track her by air. Just in case she decides to go out by Suicide Mountain. Tell you what, though. You can come over here to the Lakeside Hotel—"

"Want me to get Lena—"

"Never mind Lena. Come over here and get the key to room 22—Pepe's. Search it with a fine-tooth comb."

"For what, Sam?"

Pepe was standing near the desk. Sam looked at him as he said, "Somewhere hidden in that room I think you'll find quite a swag of money."

Pepe's face had the look of death.

2

Sam dialed a number.

"Mountain Airways. Grier speaking."

"Sam Powell, Herb. Anybody free to take up the 'copter?"

"Think you're in luck, Sam. Bill just popped into his office."

Bill Shaw owned Mountain Airways, but he still did as much air time as the two or three pilots working for him. Sam got him on the line and described the car. "She's got about a five-minute start on you. When you spot her, radio back. I'll go to the office and monitor your band."

The Lakeside Hotel was three blocks from the sheriff's offices in the Civic Building. Sam hadn't brought a car, so he walked Pepe there.

The Civic Building was a comparatively new, long single-story structure. The front portion of the building was taken up by the sheriff's offices: There was the front (reception) desk, the sheriff's outer office, a large room which served many purposes, and beyond that the private office. A long corridor stretched down the center of the building, and the other civic offices, including Sam's cubicle, opened onto this. At the far end of the corridor was a doorway downstairs to the cellblock.

"Before I take you downstairs, Pepe, is there anything you want to tell me?"

But the ex-convict had become sullen.

"Unless you want it," Sam said, "I won't book you right away. I'll give you a chance to think this thing over."

Poirier said nothing.

Sam took him down to the cellblock and turned him over to Oscar Quibell, the night janitor-jailer.

He returned to the front desk, where the powerful two-way Telefunken console was situated. There was a telephone beside the console. He dialed a number. It rang several times before:

"Hello." Deputy Curly Cameron didn't sound very enthusiastic.

"Hope I didn't wake you."

"You didn't *wake* me. No."

"Oh, oh!" Sam said. "Did I interrupt something?"

"Interrupt, be damned. You ruined it."

Sam grinned. "I apologize. Tell Shirley I apologize to her, too."

"Shirley hates you."

Sam laughed into the phone. "All kidding aside, Curly, I've got to put you to work."

"Damn!" Curly said. But he didn't argue.

"I want you to pick up Pepe Poirier's girl friend." He described the girl and the car. "She's not local, so I don't think she'll try and stick around. You drive out to that speed trap we use just before you turn off to Suicide Mountain. Bill Shaw is up in his 'copter checking to see if she's already left town. I've got the set beamed in on him. So if you want me you'll have to phone me."

"Will do."

There was a crackling of static from the small console speaker, then Bill Shaw's voice came across. "Do you read me, Sam?"

"Clear."

"I'm on the outskirts of town. Not much traffic. Shouldn't have any trouble spotting her."

Sam relaxed and lit his pipe.

Quibell came in with Poirier's clothing. Without saying anything he walked over to a large filing cabinet and placed the clothing in a drawer marked *Prisoners' Clothing.*

Quibell was about sixty, a contented bachelor. He brought out his twisted briar and lit up a bowl of Sam's tobacco.

"The young bugger was wearing a jockstrap, Sam."

Sam nodded.

"How come?"

"It's the company he keeps. Some of those people are great for playing football. When they get drinking. You know."

Oscar went "tsk tsk" sadly. "Sometimes I wish he'd quit coming back to this town. It don't do his folks any good. They get their hopes up and then he goes and does some damn fool thing again."

Sam nodded wistfully.

"Ain't two better living people in this whole valley than Alban and Herta Poirier. Why can't that young bugger stay out of trouble?"

Sam shrugged. "Recidivism, Oscar. Recidivist."

"What's that?"

"It's a high-toned word the criminologists use to describe a guy like Pepe who can't stay out of trouble."

"You still read all those big books?" Quibell asked.

"They tell us we got to keep up with the times," Sam said without enthusiasm.

"To hell with the times," Quibell said, echoing the sentiments of a good many people in Titan. Then, "What's young Poirier gone and done this time?"

"That's the problem," Sam said. "I don't know."

Oscar looked at him quizzically but asked no more questions.

As he reached the entrance to the corridor he said, "Tomorrow's Sunday. My night off. Tony's gone to Seattle for a few days." It was compulsory when there was a prisoner in a cell to have somebody on hand in the building twenty-four hours a day. Tony Deschamps was the civilian guard they used when Oscar wasn't available. "Does this mean I'm going to have to work on my night off, Sam? Baby-sit the kid?"

"No need. I'll set up the cot in my office."

"Hell, there's no need—"

"Forget it. I've got some month-end work to do anyway. I'll be here late."

Quibell disappeared down the corridor.

The speaker crackled.

Shaw's voice: "I've covered forty miles. No sign of her."

"No sense going any farther. It's clear she didn't take the big highway."

"I'll double-check on the way back, then flip over to Suicide Mountain. If she was fool enough to try to get out that way, she can't have made much time."

"If she's taking Suicide," Sam said, "I hope she's got sense enough not to *try* to make much time."

Shaw called back forty minutes later and said there was no sign of her on the mountain. Sam told him to call it a night; then, just for assurance, he phoned the state patrol in Bristow, sixty miles away, beyond the mountains, and asked them to put a pick-up on her.

"Just for questioning," he said. He told them nothing more. He didn't want the state patrol involved in Titan's affairs.

Titan looked after its own problems. Always had.

3

She had gotten out of the car to pee. He could see her squatted just beyond the open garage door. The moonlight cast her naked body in a somewhat greasy illumination. The harsh, vulgar sound of forced urination was compounded by a dull, prolonged eructation of vented flatus.

He winced. My God, what a slut.

She straightened, stood there a moment doing something to herself, then started toward him. As she reentered the darkness of the garage her high heels clicked loudly on the concrete floor. She opened the back door of the car and slid in beside him, immediately positioning herself on the seat like a well-trained bitch dog.

The confined space became heavy with the hot, musky, stale odor of her body. It should have sickened him. But emanating from this depraved wild slut of a bitch it churned at his guts and unleashed violent atavistic desires. He took her into his arms.

Her lips brushed his ear. "Did you get the money?"

Yes, he had gotten the money.

"How much?"

He had gotten her two hundred and ten dollars. It was all he had available. But it should be enough to get her started some-place.

"If I need more, can I write?"

Write! Holy mother of . . . But what if she *did* write? What if . . . Perhaps he had known it before this moment. Perhaps he had realized it from the moment she had come knocking at his door. There were just so *many* ramifications. In a fight for survival a man has to make these decisions.

"Yes. You can write."

"And you won't forget the bag," she said. "You'll be sure and get that bag. Geez, if they find . . ." Her words were choked off by a passionate intake of breath.

They clung to each other. Slowly his fingers found her throat. Very slowly. Then they locked tight. She fought him violently. But he clung to her, strangely exhilarated by this new turn of events. Then she stopped struggling. Still he clung to her throat. Perspiration stood out on his forehead; his entire body tingled in a fulminant experience of morbid gratification. Erotic hate. Primitive passion. The psychotic thrill of necrophilia.

He heard the car coming down the hill. He must hurry. He gathered the dead woman's clothes into a ball, dragged her naked body from the car, then hefted her up into his arms. He was not a large man, and her one-hundred-thirty-pound body was a burden to carry. He exited through the side door of the garage and took the winding path down to his boathouse on the edge of the lake. He unlocked the door and stepped into the boathouse just as the approaching car drove into the yard. He drew the door closed behind him. In the darkness his elbow brushed the hull of his boat. He could easily flop her into the boat, take her out onto the center of Lake Titan and dump her overboard. Her weighted body would probably never be recovered.

That was one way of doing it.

But not his way. No. In his quickly formulated plans her body must be recovered. And fairly soon.

He laid her gently on the floor, groped under his work bench until his fingers located the parabolic heater. He brought the heater out, set it near the body and turned it on. The elements heated instantly and, magnified by their specular shield, emitted an intense heat and a lurid red glow. He stared at the softly imbued body—more beautiful now than it had ever been in life. He touched the soft flesh. Warm. Very warm. And that was good. The heater would slow down the cooling processes of the body tissues, possibly confuse them as to the time of her demise. It was very fortunate that he knew about these things.

He left her then and relocked the door.

Returning up the path to the garage, he reflected upon what he had done. There was no remorse. Guilt? Why should there be? He had only done what necessity dictated. Dog eat dog. Kill or be killed. It was the homo sapiens dictum. Later he would dispose of her body. But it would be at the proper time and in the proper place.

4

Sam checked to make sure the nightlock was set on the entrance to the Civic Building, drove down to the Lakeside Hotel, and went directly to Pepe's suite. Phil Silvers charged into him and knocked him against the wall.

Deputy Silvers was nineteen years old and husky. In the past six months he had proven himself to be thorough, sharp and efficient. Shy on experience, but high in ambition. He had the makings of a first-rate lawman. But in many ways he was still a boy. And right now he evinced both embarrassment and excitement.

"Geez, Sam. I'm sorry. I . . . I was just headed down to the office. Didn't want to say anything over the hotel phone. You know. Look!" He held up a fistful of money. "I had hell's own time finding it. But I found it. Guess where I found it."

"How much there?"

"Six hundred and fifty. You'll never guess where I found it."

"Did you find anything else?"

"No. Just the money. Guess where I found it."

The boy was proud. Maybe at times a little too proud. Too much early success can make a person overly ambitious. And that can be bad. Look at Conrad Sumner, the district attorney. Was a time he was a nice, unassuming young lawyer—until he found out how smart he was. Now look at him. Hell, he'd step on his own mother's head if he thought it would put him a little closer to the top. Sumner was a disappointment to Sam. It would be unfortunate if young Silvers followed the same trail.

So Sam decided not to indulge the boy. "I have no idea *where* you found it, Phil—'less it was up the leg of the bed."

Silvers was properly deflated. "You *knew* it was there."

"No. Didn't *know*. Suspected. It's an old trick. Don't find many of those metal beds anymore. But years ago it was almost standard procedure. Pull off the caster and stick the bills up the hollow leg."

He didn't mention that he had noticed the fresh scratches on the leg where Pepe had jimmied off the caster, or that the caster hadn't been refitted quite right, thus throwing the bed slightly off level, causing it to rock when Pepe had put his weight on it.

"Why didn't you tell me it was there? Sam?"

"I figured that would be the first place you'd look," Sam said casually. Which was an out-and-out lie. But Sandy Marshal had taught him years ago that a young man learns better and remembers longer when he learns for himself.

Sam studied the money, smelled it, fingered it—thoughtfully —like you would finger a deck of cards.

"She left all her clothes, Sam. She's got beautiful duds for a whore."

"Whores like nice clothes. It's maybe the one thing that means anything to them."

"Then she must have been plenty scared—leaving them like that."

"That's her liquor glass over there. Pick up some prints. Xerox them through to Washington when you get time. See what they can tell us."

"Will do."

"But first I want you to keep searching this place."

"For what?"

"Who knows?"

"You do, Sam."

"Let's see what you can come up with."

"I want to *know*, Sam. What *exactly* am I looking for?"

Sam scowled.

But Silvers was determined. "I think I've got the right to know. I don't like this business of working in the dark all the time."

Sam's face showed his displeasure, but it was quickly replaced by a grin. However, he didn't say a word.

Silvers squirmed under Sam's relentless scrutiny, yet his determination persisted. This had obviously been eating at him for a long time. "I don't want to offend you, Sam. But I think it's only right we should discuss these things once in a while."

"All right, Phil. We can do that." His voice was without rancor. "I'm hoping maybe you'll find credit cards up here someplace."

"Why credit cards?"

"When Pepe took this money, there's an outside chance he took other things, too—like maybe credit cards—figuring to use them at a later date."

"There's nothing else up the leg of the bed. I checked it good."

"No, Pepe didn't put his money up the bed to hide it from us. He was hiding it from his girl friend."

"You mean he didn't trust her?"

"Nobody can trust a hooker, Phil. Not with money. Not with anything."

"But the thing is," Sam continued, "she was Pepe's whore. You can bet, then, that she would want her share of *all* the money. No matter *where* it came from. My own thinking is that she didn't know Pepe had this money. And he didn't want her to."

Phil looked puzzled. "Where did he get the money?"

Sam shrugged.

"But how did you know he had this money?"

"I guessed."

"Oh, come on, Sam. It had to be more than a guess."

"Well, maybe. Seemed to me when I came up here Pepe was all ready to give me some cock-and-bull story about winning a bundle of money in Vegas. I got the impression he was even prepared to show me the money—just to prove to me he wasn't over in this part of town with illegal intent.

"But when I told him I knew he came to town broke, he clammed up about having money.

"He had only twenty-five dollars in his wallet. So where was all this money he was trying to claim he won in Vegas?"

"You figure he stole it?"

"I do. He knows we're looking for money up here, will probably find it. Why didn't he tell me about the money and give me an explanation? Looks like he's willing to face a jail term for procuring rather than admit he has this money. So it's pretty conclusive that he stole it."

"Sure," Phil said. "If he gets sent up for procuring he'll likely get under five. But if he takes another rap for theft he'll probably get— God knows how long. He must be about due for the bitch list, eh?"

Sam nodded. The "bitch list" was an expression Sandy Marshal had borrowed from the Mounties up in Canada. When a man reached the bitch list he was considered to be an habitual criminal.

Sam walked over to a small writing table near the window. He opened a drawer, withdrew an envelope and wrote on it:

$650 taken from leg of bed in Pepe Poirier's room 22 Lakeside Hotel. He dated it, signed it, placed the money in it, sealed it and slid it into his shirt pocket.

"Sam, I was just thinking. Finding the money here doesn't *prove* Pepe put it here."

"Not to a judge and jury maybe."

"I'd give a lot to know where he got it."

"Yes," Sam said. "So would I."

As he was stepping out the door Silvers asked, "What the devil is *Plasto-Blast?*"

"Why do you ask?"

"There's an aerosol can of the stuff in Pepe's drawer in there."

"They use it a lot in hospitals. It's sort of a plastic bandage. They use it over incisions and cuts and scratches. You spray it on, and when it hardens it's like a layer of skin."

"Was Pepe cut up or scratched up, did you notice?"

"No."

"Maybe his girl, eh?"

"I didn't look her over real close," Sam said.

"I wonder why he keeps a can of that stuff around?"

Sam wondered the same thing.

He left the hotel and headed out of town on the big four-laner, or, as some people called it, the Prentice Freeway. Sam had his own name for it, but he kept it to himself. So far as he was concerned this four-laner was a pain in the ass. Before Senator Prentice had pulled the strings to get this thing blasted through the mountains, there had only been three ways of getting into Titan: by rail, by air and by Suicide Mountain, the latter a hair-raising experience at the best of times. Secluded by the mountains, Titan had been a world unto itself—a comfortable amount of tourist trade, a good income from the coal mines to the south of the valley, the lumber operations to the north and west, and the small ranches sprinkled all through the valley. But now, hell—now Titan, with its Lake Titan and adjoining lakes and streams, had become a tourist boom town. Everything was changing. Sam liked to think of himself as being flexible. But he wasn't convinced that all these changes were good for Titan. And it was costing the taxpayers a fortune to keep the expanding sheriff's office up to date.

His cruiser was equipped with both a telephone and a two-way radio. He radioed ahead to Curly Cameron, who was parked in the speed trap.

No, Curly told him, no sign of the Mink girl or her car.

Ten minutes later Sam had backed his cruiser off the highway, into the trees, and was parked beside Curly. It was 1:30 A.M.

Curly Cameron was twenty-nine years old and good-looking in a blond he-man sort of way. He had worked with Sam for six years and Sam liked him.

Sam told him he would take over now.

"You going to sit out here all night?"

"Why not? I don't have a wife waiting for me."

"I hope the hell *I* do," Curly quipped. Then, "Do you think the girl will still try to get out of town tonight?"

"I doubt it. She acts like a pretty cute operator or she'd have tried to get out right away. Chances are she'll wait now and try to move out in the heavy Sunday traffic."

"My guess is she's probably parked the car in some trees and is sleeping in it."

"Could be," Sam said. "But a hooker likes her comfort."

"You want me to check the hotels and motels?"

"Not tonight. You go home now. I promise not to ring the telephone."

"That bloody phone. It was Shirley's idea to put it by the bed. She's going to have it moved soon as she gets back from Bristow."

"She going to Bristow?"

"First thing in the morning. That's why tonight was sort of important. She's going to be gone a week. Her sister is having a baby."

"Well, you get the hell home, then," Sam said.

When Curly had gone, Sam took a two-hundred foot roll of very small pneumatic hose from the trunk of the cruiser. Unrolling it, he walked along the edge of the highway toward Titan. When he reached the end of the hose he carried it out onto the highway and laid it across the two lanes coming from Titan. He returned to the car. Attached to this end of the hose was a small bell. He rolled down a back window and placed the bell and a short section of the hose inside. Any car coming from Titan would ring the bell twice: first when the front wheels crossed the hose, again when the rear wheels crossed.

There was very little traffic on the road.

Sam placed his binoculars on the seat beside him, closed his eyes and immediately dozed off.

SUNDAY

1

The sound of the bell persisted—monotonous, irritating.

She awoke, groggy. Then was instantly alert, realizing the phone had been ringing for quite a while. She got out of bed, snuggled her feet into a pair of fluffy blue slippers, and headed for the stairway.

Justine Marshal coming downstairs in a short nightie was something to see. Her long hair, assiduously combed the night before, framed her face and abounded at her shoulders like a shimmering Titian cloud. The black nightie, well up on her thighs, accented the geometrical perfection of her long, slender legs.

The fragrance of freshly brewed coffee wafted up the stairway and she wondered why her mother or Frieda hadn't answered the phone.

She lifted the receiver. "Justine Marshal speaking."

"Sheriff, this is Mrs. Kit Belman." The voice was sharp and unfriendly.

"What can I do for you, Mrs. Belman?"

"For me? Nothing. I'm afraid, however, I have some unfortunate news. About fifteen minutes ago my husband and I were motoring along Tower Mountain and came across a smashed automobile. It had gone off the road and smashed into the trees below. My husband says that Larry Prentice is in the car and that he is dead."

"Was he alone?"

"Yes."

"Have you notified anyone else?"

"I have had enough difficulty," she replied, "notifying you."

"Suicide Mou——" Justine caught herself. Trixie Belman belonged to the school who believed the name "Suicide Mountain" was bad for the tourist business. As president of the chamber of commerce she did everything possible to abolish the use of the sobriquet. It was a stubborn, useless effort, but Justine didn't wish to offend her. Trixie Belman was hostile enough as it was. "Tower Mountain. Where exactly, Mrs. Belman?"

"You will find our car parked at the spot."

"Thank you, Mrs. Belman."

So ended the charmed and useless life of Larry Randolph Prentice. But it had taken some doing. He had come out of three prior accidents miraculously unharmed. Son of Titan's wealthiest merchant—and nephew of the senator—he had lived a high, useless, playboy existence. No one had held him in much esteem. Except of course his father, Hector Prentice. And, perhaps, his wife Pat and their two children.

She waited until Trixie Belman broke the connection, then she immediately began dialing Sam Powell's number. She had the number half dialed before she caught herself. "No, damn it," she said aloud, "*I'm* the sheriff."

She quickly dressed in jodhpurs, checked shirt, jacket and riding boots—suitable attire for mountain work. She tied her long hair in a ribbon, then phoned Dr. Blainsworth, the coroner, and Billy Badger, the local photographer.

Passing through the kitchen, she noticed a note propped up on the table.

> *Wilbur's home from hospital. Frieda and I have*
> *gone next door to make breakfast for him and*
> *Bobby.*
>
>   *AIDA*

She glanced wistfully at the pot of coffee brewing on the stove, then left the house.

The going was tricky on Suicide Mountain. She found Trixie Belman's Cadillac convertible parked at the outer edge of the road. A short distance behind it was a shiny red Italian sports car which she recognized as belonging to Henry Pike, owner of the The Henry Pike, one of Titan's newest resort hotels.

Trixie Belman sat at the wheel of the convertible. She wore sunglasses. Her hair was cut short and tightly coiffured. She made a point of glancing at her wrist watch as Justine approached, then indicated a point beyond the edge of the road near the front of the Cadillac. "My husband and Henry Pike are down there now."

Justine walked to the edge of the road and looked down into the tops of trees which stretched below in a steep slope for a thousand feet. From where she stood she couldn't see Prentice's car. But she could see where some small trees had been broken, and she could see footprints in the earth. She followed them downward, grasping at bushes and trees to control her momentum. She hadn't traveled far when she came upon the wrecked car. It had been virtually concealed from the road by some heavy bushes which had sprung back into place after the vehicle passed through.

Kit Belman and Henry Pike stood near the wreckage. Both men looked pale and uncomfortable.

Larry Prentice's car in its downward plunge had ripped out several trees, finally coming to rest with its nose twisted around a huge pine. Although every window had shattered out, indicating that the car had probably rolled at least once on its descent, the doors had miraculously remained closed and Prentice's body still sat hunched over the wheel. His body seemed to have swollen in death, causing his shoulders to press out against the seams of his expensive suit, making the suit appear much too small.

As she moved close to Prentice to study his position at the wheel something caught her attention, causing her to take an involuntary step backward. She stared apprehensively at the hard leather-brown horizontal marks in the skin around Prentice's neck just above the collar.

She licked her lips nervously, then turned to the two men. Neither seemed inclined to come any nearer to the car.

"You found the car, Kit?"

Kit Belman nodded. "My wife, actually. By pure chance. We were out bird watching and we had lost a hubcap from our automobile. We were driving along, hoping against hope to find it. My wife noticed the reflection of the sun on the metal of the car. I came down. This is what I found."

Belman gave this account in a dignified, matter-of-fact, supercilious manner. He stood very erect as he spoke; he always stood erect, thereby making himself appear taller than his five feet, seven inches. He was in his mid-thirties; his sandy hair, graying at the temples, gave him a dignified appearance which he no doubt enjoyed. Kit made a good husband to Trixie. He was every bit as determined as she was that he should get ahead, be somebody. And in eight years he had risen from a public school teacher to principal of the Titan County School Unit. A position of prominence in the valley. For a boy who had started with absolutely nothing, he had accomplished much. And with that accomplishment had come arrogance.

"Did you happen to touch anything, Kit?" Justine asked.

She considered it a basic, routine question, but it caused Belman to stiffen indignantly. "I'm aware that one does not disturb an accident scene. I ascertained that the man was dead by feeling his forehead, then I had my wife go to a phone and contact you."

"I appreciate it." She turned to Henry. "And you, Henry?"

"No. I was driving some distance behind the Belmans. I saw

their car parked, so I decided to stop and see what was going on. I'm sorry," he added, "that this is what we found."

"If you don't need us for anything further, my wife and I will be on our way," Belman said.

She glanced again at the marks on Prentice's neck. "Very well."

"Anything I can do?" Pike asked.

"Perhaps if you stay up on the road, Henry, and show Doc Blainsworth and Billy Badger where to come when they get here . . ."

When the two men had gone she resumed her investigation. She studied Prentice's hands. There was a good deal of dead skin and traces of blood under the nails. She attempted to raise Prentice's head. In the process her eye caught something colorful in the back seat. A distinctive lavender-colored fabric almost concealed by scattered newspapers and a throw rug. She reached in through the broken window and pushed the newspapers aside.

It was a small lavender cosmetics case.

The sight of it gave her a start. Gingerly, apprehensively, she lifted the case from the car. There was a gold-embossed *B* on the bag. Her face became very pale.

"My God!" she said.

Carrying the cosmetics case, she started up the steep incline to the road. Henry Pike stood near his sports car patiently smoking a cigarette.

"No sign of them yet, sheriff."

She attempted to use her body to shield the case from Pike's view. But she lost her footing and had to throw her arms up to regain her balance. Pike glanced at the case but showed little apparent interest in it.

She placed the case in the trunk of her cruiser and was just closing the trunk when a car drew to a stop behind her.

It was Sam Powell.

2

At 9:10 that morning Sam had been alerted from a half-sleep by two very rapid "clangs" from the bell hung in the back seat of his car. The spacing of the two sounds indicated that a car had passed over the pneumatic hose at an excessive speed. He was surprised when he recognized it as an official car from the sheriff's office. And even more surprised to see Justine at the wheel.

He put the glasses on her as she swung off the highway and started up Suicide Mountain. She was traveling much too fast for the conditions of that road. He reached for the microphone on the two-way radio, then changed his mind. If she had wanted him she would have contacted him. Still he was puzzled. And troubled.

There was a time when Sam and Justine had been very close. But that was a long time ago, it seemed. Since she had returned from Los Angeles—where she had worked with the L.A. police department—and become sheriff of Titan, things had not gone nearly so well as Sam had hoped. It wasn't that she had curtailed his authority, because she hadn't. Not a whole lot, anyway. (Although she was at times erratic about this and frequently gave him the impression that she thought he was overstepping his mark.) But what bothered him was the defensive wall she had set between them. It made for an uneasy situation.

After arguing with himself for several minutes, he phoned Phil Silvers to come and relieve him. Without waiting for Phil he took off for Suicide Mountain.

He drew to a stop behind Justine's car and got out.

She gave him only the very briefest of glances. "There's been an accident." Her voice was cold. She withdrew a black paraphernalia kit from her car, crossed the road and disappeared down the slope on the other side.

He was troubled by her hostile greeting. He could read her like a book. She was obviously very upset. Did his uninvited appearance antagonize her that much?

He strolled casually across to Henry Pike, who was standing beside his sports car.

"What's the trouble, Henry?"

The hotel owner fidgeted with the doeskin driving gloves he held in his hands. He was a tall man in his early forties, balding, with dark hair. He was a comparative newcomer to Titan. With his sports cars and his high living he was indicative of the type of person the new four-laner was bringing to the valley.

"Larry Prentice went over the edge in his car and killed himself."

Sam looked very closely into Pike's face, gauging the man's emotions. Pike, he knew, had played a lot of poker with Prentice.

"You see it happen, Henry?"

"No."

Sam walked to the edge of the road and looked down. Justine was disappearing into some trees a short distance below. But he could not see Prentice's car.

He studied the edge of the road beyond the pavement until he found tire tracks going over the edge. They had been made in mud and had dried, distinct and unmarked. The tracks indicated that the car had been coming from up-mountain. Prentice had a mountain retreat about three miles up the road.

Sam frowned. He studied the tracks more carefully. He obviously didn't like what he saw.

He called Pike over. "See that nobody touches those tire tracks, Henry. I don't want them disturbed."

He returned to his cruiser and phoned deputy Seymour Dinsmore. "I know it's your day off, Seymour. But we've got an accident up here on Suicide Mountain. I want the area staked off as out of bounds and the slope searched carefully."

He started down the slope. There was nothing about his big frame to indicate he had any great agility. But he had been born and raised in these mountains. He descended the slope with the speed and the skill of a Sherpa.

He caught up with Justine before she reached the car.

"Looks like it happened sometime very early Friday morning," he said.

"I imagine if he had been missing that long we would have heard about it."

"He was supposed to be out of town on business."

"Maybe."

"He was either dead drunk or asleep when it happened."

She stopped in her tracks. "Why did you say that?"

"The tracks up there. No indication that he tried to turn the front wheels or that he even applied his brakes."

"Larry was a reckless driver. Isn't there the possibility he was traveling so fast he didn't have *time* to apply his brakes?"

"You haven't studied the tracks, Justine?"

"No."

"The car was traveling at *no speed at all* when it went off the road. Otherwise, the impetus would have carried it far out over the edge, and it wouldn't have struck the slope for several hundred feet. But the tracks show that the car just sort of tipped over the edge. No impetus behind it at all."

Despite the exertion of descending the slope, Justine's face was unnaturally pale. She was extremely upset and she wasn't concealing it very well.

Sam believed in bringing things out into the open. "Justine, what's wrong?"

"Wrong?"

"Something's bothering you. I want to know what."

"All right, then. I think Larry Prentice was murdered. I think he was choked to death."

"And?"

"And! For God's sake!" she exclaimed. Her voice was louder than necessary and nervously keyed. "Isn't that enough?"

No. It wasn't enough. Murder wasn't an everyday occurrence in Titan County. But Justine was made out of stronger stuff than this. However, Sam didn't pursue it further.

They reached the wrecked car.

He noted the horizontal leathery choke marks in the skin around Prentice's neck.

With considerable effort he managed to raise Prentice's head from the wheel. Larry Prentice was no longer the handsome man he had been. His face was badly smashed by the accident. The movement of larvae at the corners of his mouth and in his eyes indicated he had been dead at least two days.

Justine was studying the face. She seemed to have better control of herself. "It looks as though you could be right about the time of the accident," she said. "How did you arrive at 'Friday morning'?"

"The tire tracks were made in mud. Our last rain was Thursday night. It rained pretty hard till about midnight, then let up to a drizzle for a while. If the tracks had been made during the heavy part of that rain, they would have been washed away. And they had to be made before the sun came out and dried the earth."

She nodded. "The light switch is pulled out. So the lights were on."

The windshield wiper control was at the "on" position.

She said, "It looks as though it happened while it was still drizzling out."

"Probably between midnight and twelve-thirty."

He studied the corpse. The body seemed to have swollen in the suit. The top button on the shirt was undone. There was also a button missing from the front of the shirt. Further, one of the cuff links was on backwards.

The picture was all wrong. Prentice had always flaunted his good looks and immaculate appearance.

"Looks like somebody *else* dressed him," Sam said. "Larry wouldn't wear a shirt with a button missing or put a cuff link on backwards."

"He has a cottage up the road three or four miles," she said. "It could be he was in bed when he was attacked."

"A good possibility."

"But if he was supposed to be out of town on business," she said, "what was he doing up in his cottage?"

"That," Sam replied, "is a real good question."

He studied the dead hands—the shredded skin and dried blood under the fingernails. "Looks like he scratched his killer up pretty good."

"Or else we're supposed to *think* he did," she said.

She opened her black paraphernalia kit. It contained various items of investigative equipment. Sam watched her as she took the scrapings from under Prentice's fingernails and placed them in a glass tube which she carefully labeled. She removed hairs clinging to the suit and placed them in another tube. She pulled samples of hair from Prentice's head.

When she had finished, Sam went through the pockets of the suit. He found a neatly written note:

> *Darling,*
> *I'll meet you in the lounge at about 5 P.M. I'll*
> *think of some excuse. Please don't forget me.*
>   *B*

He reread the note, pondered over it for several seconds.

"What is it?" she asked.

He handed it to her, watched for her reaction.

She read it, quickly turned away. But not completely. Half turned, she stopped, took another, closer look at the note. She continued to study the note for some time, obviously lost in thought. Making a point of not facing Sam, she knelt down, placed the note between two sheets of glass, applied a small red clamp to hold the two pieces of glass together, and set them carefully into her black paraphernalia kit.

"Well?" Sam asked.

"Well what?"

"The note. How do you see it?"

"I'm thinking." She was still kneeling over the kit, her back to him. "It would seem to simplify things considerably for us."

"Would seem to," Sam agreed.

"We know that Larry wouldn't carry a note like this in his pocket where his wife might find it. So he must have received this note shortly before he left town on Thursday. All we do is ask around at the lounges to find out who he was drinking with Thursday afternoon and we'll find the *B* who wrote this letter. Maybe then . . ." She stood up and turned to face him. "It's a starting point, Sam."

"Yes," he agreed. But somehow he had the feeling she didn't really believe in this note. And something about that note bothered him, too. But at the moment something else bothered him even more. "Justine," he said, "there's no wallet."

"No wallet?" She frowned. "That *could* change the entire complexion of this."

He said nothing.

"Don't you agree? . . . Sam?"

"I don't know what to think. This looks like a bungle from start to finish. Or maybe it just *looks* that way. No great effort was made to make it look like an accident. The killer took the wallet and left the note. . . . I don't know, Justine."

"Don't you place any importance on the missing wallet?"

"I do. But I'm not sure what. This just doesn't have the earmarks of a robbery."

Doc Blainsworth and Billy Badger arrived. Billy took pictures of the note and various other important aspects of the accident, then Doc Blainsworth began his examination.

Sam and Justine ascended to the road.

A car screeched to a stop. The door flew open and Conrad Sumner, the district attorney, leaped out and charged toward them fuming, his tall, thin body trembling.

"Why wasn't I notified of this?" he cried. "Why?"

Sam smiled at him and patted him playfully on the shoulder. "It's all right, Connie. We figured we could somehow manage it on our own."

Sumner glared at him, pivoted and started down the slope.

"Connie," Sam called.

Sumner stopped, glanced back over his shoulder. "What?"

"Don't disturb anything down there."

Sumner's face became livid. He said something under his breath and turned away.

"I love the way you deflate that pompous ass," Justine said.

And in the next breath she was all business. "Get a moulage of these tire tracks, Sam. And some pictures. I'll go on up to Larry's cottage."

"Want me to come up when I'm finished?"

"If you wish."

She had trouble starting her car. Without saying anything Sam walked across to give her a hand. And immediately wished he hadn't.

At the sound of his footsteps she turned. There were tears in her eyes. She was crying.

Sam pretended not to notice. He lifted the hood and jiggled the corroded connection on the positive post of the battery. The car started. She drove away without thanking him or looking at him.

A station wagon drew up a short distance down the road. It was Schuyler Kleinfeld, the newscaster, in his vividly lettered *Living News* car. Kleinfeld got out carrying a tape machine. He was accompanied by a TV photographer. They pretended not to see Sam and headed directly for the edge of the road. Sam stuck thumb and little finger in his mouth and emitted a shrill, piercing whistle. They couldn't ignore that, and when they looked his way he held up his hand for them to stop.

He walked casually over to them. Kleinfeld was an eager beaver and he was fairly dancing to get down that hill. He chewed impatiently on his big cigar. He was not the type that suited a cigar. But he always smoked one—his projected image of the big time.

"Out of bounds, Sky."

"Ah, come on now, Sam. For cryin' out loud. We've got as much . . ." He sensed he was overstepping his mark, so he let it drop. Making a new start and in a nicer tone he asked, "When can we, Sam?"

"When we've finished our investigation."

"About when?"

"Maybe tomorrow. Maybe today. I'll give you a call."

"Give me a *call!*"

"Back your wagon down the road another fifty yards. No closer, Sky."

"But what's the sense of having a TV–radio operation in this town if . . . "

Sam had turned and walked away. A couple of minutes later the wagon came to life and slowly backed down the road the required distance.

An hour later Sam arrived at Prentice's cottage, secluded, well off the road. This had been Prentice's sanctum sanctorum. His wife Pat and the two children seldom came here. He used it when he had work to do, or when he wished to be alone. Or so the story went.

The entire area had been concreted, so there were no tracks from the night of the rain.

Justine stood in the doorway. There was no longer any indication she had been crying.

"I found the missing shirt button," she said. "It was near the bed. There are several suits of clothing in the closet. But no wallet.

"The place is almost completely free of fingerprints. Somebody has obviously taken pains to remove them. Photograph what prints there are."

She started toward her car and stopped. "The bed hasn't been made. You'll find semen stains on the sheet."

"How about hairs?"

"Yes," she said. "I found two pubic hairs—I assume they're pubic hairs."

"Prentice's, do you think?"

"How the devil would *I* know *whose* they are?"

"What I mean is: Prentice is light-complexioned; his hair is very blond. Were these hairs—?"

"No," she said. "They are very dark."

She reached her car. "I'm going down to notify his wife."

"Justine . . . do you want me to look after that end?"

"No. It's my responsibility."

"Better let her think it was an accident," he suggested. "Matter of fact, we better keep it to ourselves just as long as we possibly can."

"Yes," she said. "I know what you mean."

He watched her leave. She seemed so slender and fragile. He felt sorry for her.

Hector Prentice's son had been murdered. There was going to be hell to pay.

3

It was early evening when Sam returned to town. Using his mobile phone he called ahead to the hospital, then drove right on over. Doc Blainsworth did his autopsy work in the morgue downstairs. Sam found him in a small office outside the autopsy room.

Blainsworth was a rotund sixty-five and looked older. He had been both coroner and medical examiner in Titan for as long as Sam could remember. He obviously enjoyed the post, but it was doubtful that he could resign even if he wanted to; he was a tradition in the valley, just as Sandy Marshal had been a tradition. And Titan—like most rural areas long cut off from the mainstream—was strong on tradition endemic to its own local self and not readily amenable to change. Doc was an irascible, caustic, independent old codger. But he and Sam got along just fine. He was in his shirt sleeves smoking a cigar. There was blood between his fingers and on his wrists.

"*Kee*-rist," he said. "You look like I feel. I've had the whole Prentice family on my back all afternoon wanting to see the cadaver."

"Did you tell them you were doing an autopsy?"

"I didn't tell them nothing. But that Hector Prentice just won't take no. He's on the board of directors of the hospital and I've spent more time arguing with officials than working. I finally told them to stick the hospital up their ass. That's when they left me alone."

"What did you find, Doc?"

Blainsworth frowned. "Didn't you see the report?"

"Just got back into town."

"Well, our suspicions were confirmed. He was dead before the accident. Choked to death by human hands."

"Any indication he was drugged or drunk?"

"No. Mind you, he had been drinking. His blood had eight-hundredths percent alcohol. Which is maybe three average drinks. That wouldn't make him drunk."

"Then there's not much chance he was killed by a woman."

"No chance, I'd say. Leastways no average woman. Certainly not the kind of women he screwed around with. It took a pretty fair pair of hands to do that job."

"Why do you say that?"

"The windpipe was completely collapsed. And, oh, yeh—here's something else for you to think about. There is considerable dried semen on his genitals, all over his penis and matted in the pubic hair. Which looks to these rheumy old eyes as though somebody caught him at it right after his ejaculation and killed him before he had a chance to wipe himself off."

"Did you put that in your report, Doc?"

"Naw. Nothing about the semen. I notated it in my own book, but figured I could always add it to your report later if you decided you wanted it for the record."

Sam grinned—almost. Talk about unconventional! Old Doc and Sandy Marshal had made quite a pair. But there weren't many of the old mavericks left. They were systematically being removed by the attrition of an encroaching society which made no allowance for the nonconformist; either in medicine or in law.

"How long can you hold off the inquest?" Sam asked.

"Hell, Sumner was feeling me out to see if we might avoid an inquest altogether."

"Sumner? Does *he* suspect it wasn't an accident?"

"I gave him the report to take over to your— Oh, oh! A mistake, eh?"

Sam nodded.

"Jesus, I'm sorry. I never thought. I figured, him being the district attorney ... "

"It's my fault, Doc. I should have warned you down at the accident. I was hoping we'd get a day or two to work on it before word got out it wasn't an accident."

"Sumner's on the Prentice team. He won't blab."

"He won't blab, Doc. But it's pretty safe to assume that Hector Prentice knows about it right now."

"And that's what you *didn't* want. Right?"

"He's a merciless son of a bitch. You know that. He'll want this solved. But he won't want scandal. The way I see it, there's going to be a hell of a scandal before this is finished. I'm a little concerned as to what kind of pressure he's going to bear down with, and just how much influence he really has."

"He has no influence with me," Blainsworth stated, then asked, "How about Sandy's girl? What kind of stuff is she made of?"

"Justine is a smart girl."

"I've known Aida all my life. And I liked Sandy. But I admit I never got to know the kid very well. Is she another Sandy Marshal?"

"There was only one of those," Sam said.

Blainsworth nodded thoughtfully. "Then maybe you'll have to run interference for her. Just how bad a scandal do you see in this?"

"Larry was supposedly out of town on business. Instead of that he was out at his cottage. Seems pretty obvious he was seducing somebody's woman when he was killed."

"Any idea who?"

Sam nodded. "An idea. Not a very pleasant idea, but ... That's the price of the job."

Blainsworth leaned forward in his chair. "I know you don't like to discuss these things ..."

Sam nodded.

"However," he continued, "if I'm going to run interference here, maybe I should be let in on it."

"It's only a suspicion. Maybe we'd better—"

"Your suspicions have an uncanny habit of bearing fruit."

Sam said nothing.

Blainsworth leaned back in his chair. "I don't mind cooperating, Sam. But damn it, boy, I don't want to be kept in the dark. Not on something like this."

The two men stared at each other.

"All right, Doc." He sat down, drew out his pipe. "How well do you know Wilbur Hancock?"

Blainsworth frowned. "Wilbur? Hell, I've known him all his life; brought him into this world." He scowled. "Christ! You're not suggesting that Wilbur—? Hell, Wilbur would no more kill a man than . . . than . . ."

"Than what?" Sam asked. "Than try to commit suicide?"

Blainsworth closed his eyes. "Jesus H. Christ!"

Sam sucked at his pipe. He wasn't enjoying any part of this and his face showed it.

Doc rubbed his eyes. "It just didn't make sense—Wilbur trying suicide. Hell, it wasn't the first time his wife had run out on him. That tramp played poor Wilbur for a sucker from the day they met. But suicide? No. Yet, if what you say is true—yes. All of a sudden it makes sense."

"It's only a suspicion, Doc."

"How do you think it happened?"

"Barbara ran out on Wilbur. He must have known she was buggering around with Larry Prentice. He went up to Prentice's cabin and caught them at it."

"That would explain it!" Doc agreed. "It's one thing to suspect your wife is cheating on you. It's another thing to *find* her bedded with another man. Sure. Wilbur lost his temper. He's strong as a horse. He could choke to death a man like Prentice without really meaning to."

"We scraped a lot of blood and skin from under Prentice's fingernails."

"Which could explain those scratches on Wilbur's face."

Sam nodded.

"Was there enough blood to get a type on it?"

"I think so."

Blainsworth wore a troubled expression. "How's the girl taking this?"

"The girl?"

"The sheriff. Justine."

"We haven't discussed it."

"Does she know you suspect Wilbur?"

"We haven't discussed it."

"This is going to put her in one *hell* of a position—Wilbur being her cousin, Gertie being her mother's sister."

"If it turns out Wilbur is guilty, I'll take the responsibility for it off her shoulders."

"It's a sad son of a bitch of a situation," Blainsworth said.

Sam nodded.

Blainsworth rubbed his forehead. He looked a hundred years old. Very softly he said, "Be sure of your ground, Sam. Be goddamned sure of it before you make your next move. Because, just as sure as I'm sitting here, the day you arrest Wilbur for murder is the day I'll have to sign the death certificate for his mother."

Sam's strong, square face concealed any emotions he might be experiencing.

Blainsworth faced him squarely, spoke deliberately. "Gertie has a good constitution, and when she found out Wilbur was still alive it gave her new life. She's coming right along, Sam." He leaned forward in his chair. The suggestion was very evident in his voice as he continued. "Give her a while—a few weeks, even a few days could make the difference—and her heart will be in pretty fair shape again." He hesitated. "But—throw another shock at her now and . . ." He spread his arms in a hopeless gesture, then waited for something from Sam.

But the lawman remained stubbornly silent, his impassive gray eyes offering nothing at all.

"Damn it, boy! Justice is blind. Sometimes it's *too* damned blind. It's the responsibility of men like you to temper it. Hell, you worked with Sandy long enough—"

Sam stood up. "My hands are tied, Doc." He shook his head sadly but determinedly.

"Tied be damned! What do you suppose Sandy Marshal would have done in a case like this?"

"Exactly what I'm doing."

"Even if it meant killing his wife's sister? Bullshit! Christ, I'm not telling you to let Wilbur go scot free. All I'm asking is that you *wait*. Drag it out—delay it—wait until Gertie is on her feet, strong enough to take the blow."

"Normally that might be possible. But not this time."

"Why?"

"Because Hector Prentice and Connie Sumner won't give me the chance."

"The hell they won't! Hector Prentice will move mountains to avoid this scandal. And the senator right behind him. Hell, I'll stake my practice on the fact that Hector would sooner see Wilbur go scot free than have it come out that his son was killed while sleeping with Barbara Hancock."

"That's my point," Sam said. "They'll grab at any straw they can get to avoid scandal. And unfortunately I've got a ready-made patsy waiting for them down in the cellblock. Pepe Poirier. He had six hundred and fifty dollars he couldn't account for. Add to that the fact that Larry Prentice's wallet is missing. Exactly the sort of straw Connie Sumner would jump at.

"If I sat back, withholding evidence while all this was going on, and then later presented my evidence showing Wilbur to be guilty—I would be ruined; Justine would be ruined. Hector Prentice would have the state police in here running this town within twenty-four hours. The sheriff's office would be a thing of the past in this county."

Blainsworth considered Sam's words, nodded his understanding, then suggested, "Isn't there some chance of a deal—an arrangement—with Sumner?"

"No chance. Sandy tried that once and almost got crucified."

"Piss of a setup, if you ask me," Blainsworth said.

Sam started for the door, then stopped. "I noticed Wilbur's car parked out front. Is he visiting his mother?"

"Probably. You're not figuring to go up there and ... ?"

"When are visiting hours over?"

"You're not going to arrest him *today,* for chrissake?"

"Doc, I won't touch Wilbur till I know beyond all doubt that he's guilty. Right now I've just got suspicions."

"Let's hope those suspicions don't amount to bugger all." He glanced at his watch. "Visiting hours are over in ten minutes."

Sam was stepping through the door when Blainsworth said, "Hey! Don't forget these." He held up a clear plastic bag filled with clothing. "Larry Prentice's clothes."

Sam gathered up the bag and was again stepping through the door when Blainsworth asked, "Where's Barbara Hancock now?"

"That," Sam said, "is a real good question."

4

Sam went to his cruiser, placed Prentice's clothes in the trunk and locked it.

Then he went over to Wilbur's car. The key was in the ignition. Sam shook his head. Wasn't that just like Wilbur. He unlocked Wilbur's trunk and let the air out of the spare tire. Then he circled to a front tire and let the air out of it.

He was sitting in his cruiser a short distance away when Wilbur came out of the hospital. Wilbur noticed the flat front tire immediately, opened the trunk and took out the spare. When he realized the spare was also flat he picked it up and started downtown with it.

Sam drew the cruiser up beside him and stopped. "Lift, Wilbur?"

Wilbur looked at him, then looked away. "No. 'S all right. I can walk."

Sam pushed the door open. "Hop in. No sense walking. . . . Just throw the tire in the back seat."

Wilbur was obviously ill at ease.

"Doc Blainsworth tells me your mother's coming along real good."

"Yuh."

"You gave her quite a scare."

Wilbur said nothing.

"I guess you know I've got to ask you a few questions."

"Why?"

"It's part of the business, Wilbur."

"What kind of questions?"

"About your accident, how you got gassed by the exhaust fumes. I've got to find out how it came to happen."

"Justine's already asked me them questions."

"When was that?"

"This morning."

"Oh. Then I won't have to ask you. No sense in asking the same questions twice."

Wilbur seemed relieved.

"I imagine Justine asked you how you got those scratches on your face?"

"She asked me all them questions."

"What did you tell her?"

"I guess it ain't no secret. Barbara and I had a fight."

"Your wife scratched you?"

"Yes."

"Justine drove your wife to the bus depot Thursday afternoon. Any idea where she went?"

"No."

"Have you heard from her?"

"No."

"Did she have much money?"

"I don't know. She looked after the house money. Whatever it was—she took it."

Sam dropped him off at a filling station. A mechanic took the tire, and Wilbur followed him to the back. Sam went to the

attendant at the front desk. "When the tire's fixed, drive Wilbur
back to the hospital. Charge it to the sheriff's office."

Back in the cruiser he phoned Wilbur's house. No answer.

He drove to within a quarter block of Wilbur's house, then
walked. The door was unlocked. He went directly to the
kitchen. There was a note on the table.

> *Wilbur:*
> *Bobby is with me. Come on across and have*
> *coffee and cookies with us.*
>
> AIDA

What Sam was looking for was a copy of Barbara Hancock's handwriting. He searched the cupboard until he
found the recipe drawer. The recipes had been written by
several different people. At length he found something that
satisfied him. A recipe had been written on the back of
this note:

> *Wilbur:*
> *I'll be late. There's hamburger in the fridge. If*
> *Bobby's peed himself again there should be*
> *clean underwear in the clothes basket in the*
> *basement.*
>
> BABS

Sam studied the handwriting carefully, then folded the note
and placed it in his shirt pocket. It was only then that he realized he was still carrying the $650 that had been taken from
Pepe Poirier's hotel room.

He drove slowly toward the Civic Building. He was tired and
his thoughts were not very pleasant. He was virtually certain
that the note in his pocket and the note they had found in
Prentice's pocket had been written by the same person. Barbara Hancock. A heartbreaking situation. He felt deep compassion for Gertie in the hospital. And little Bobby. This was one

of those situations that oftentimes made his job pretty hard to stomach.

And Justine was caught right in the middle. A dirty twist, that.

Chances were she had already compared the handwriting.

As he drew up near the front of the Civic Building, Alban and Herta Poirier were just leaving. They didn't see him. He unlocked the trunk and retrieved the plastic bag containing Prentice's clothes and the carefully folded bed sheet from the cottage.

Justine was in her private office. She looked worn and haggard and—beautiful. And, as always, she seemed so fragile and out of place behind that big desk which had been specially made for Sandy Marshal. The whole office was Sandy. The prize antelope head, the deer head with the four-foot rack he had shot up in northern Canada, the citation from the governor, the sharp-shooting awards, even the gold-plated cuspidor which had been presented to Sandy forty years ago by a visiting English nobleman. She had changed nothing, obviously considering herself to be no more than a continuation or extension of her father. To Sam this was bad. But none of his business.

"How did Pat Prentice take her husband's death?" he asked.

"She didn't take it well."

"I've got Prentice's clothes here. And the bed sheet. What drawer are you keeping the evidence in?"

"The one with the key in the lock."

He opened the filing cabinet drawer and carefully placed the plastic bag on top of the other items.

"And this money I got from Pepe's hotel room. Where should I put it?"

"I'm wondering if we won't end up putting it in that same drawer."

He didn't like that remark at all. "You're kidding, of course."

But she didn't say she was kidding; she didn't say anything.

He unlocked the drawer next to the Prentice drawer and placed the envelope of money in there. He went to a chair and sat down. He waited for Justine to open the conversation, but she seemed disinclined to.

"I see Alban and Herta were here. What did they want?"

"To see their son, of course. And I let them."

Something in Sam's expression must have annoyed her, for she flared right up. "Is there any crime in their seeing their son?"

He looked at her a long moment. But she did not look at him. He stood up. "I'll be right back." He went to his office and got a small bottle of liquor from a drawer. He picked up a couple of paper cups on the way back.

"What's this all about?" she asked.

"I think we could both use a good belt."

She didn't argue. And when he poured her a stiff one she didn't say stop. She drank it straight.

"All we need now," she said, "is for Hector Prentice to walk in here and catch us boozin' it up."

"Has Hector tried to contact you?"

"No."

"If Hector Prentice sticks his nose in here tonight, I'll give you the pleasure of kicking his ass clear out to the street."

That almost brought a smile to her lips.

"Any new developments?" he asked tentatively.

She pushed a tendril of hair from in front of her eyes. "Where do we start?" she sighed.

He frowned. That was not the answer he had expected. Not at all.

He asked, "Have you had a chance yet to compare the handwriting?"

"What handwriting?"

"The note. The note we found in Larry Prentice's pocket."

"Compare it with what, pray tell?"

Sam was floored by her answer. *Compare it with what, pray tell!* He fought hard to conceal his reaction. There was no doubt in his mind that she had suspected Wilbur. For some reason she had suspected him even *before* they had discovered the note; that explained her strange behavior when he had arrived unexpectedly at the scene of the murder. And the tears she had shed later—after they had discovered the note—only clinched his suspicions.

Hell—everything pointed to Wilbur. She couldn't have missed it. And he knew that she hadn't missed it: Justine was anything but a fool. The fact that she had already questioned Wilbur left no doubt where her suspicions lay.

Was there any chance that Doc Blainsworth had gotten to her and influenced her reasoning, persuaded her to throw a wrench into the works and deliberately draw out the investigation? It was something the old devil might do if it meant the possibility of saving Gertie's life. And if, indeed, this was her intention, then she was making an irrevocable mistake.

". . . after all," she was saying, "this is Sunday. The lounges are closed. If Larry Prentice had an assignation with some woman in one of the lounges, we won't be able to check fully on it until tomorrow."

Sam decided to pull no punches. Best straighten this mess out right now before it got beyond straightening. "Justine," he said, "I think we should compare that note with Barbara Hancock's writing."

She looked at him narrowly. "Do you consider me *that* incompetent, Sam?"

"I don't consider you incompetent at all."

"Then what *are* you thinking? Don't you think I considered the possibility that Wilbur might have killed Larry Prentice?"

"You talked to him?"

"Yes."

"And he has an alibi for Thursday night?"

"His mother will be his alibi, Sam. We'll have to wait until she is in fit condition before I dare question her. But I believe everything Wilbur told me. Everything."

"Justine . . . when I asked earlier whether you had compared the handwriting, you gave me the impression you didn't know what to compare it with."

"And I didn't. And I don't."

"But you compared it with Barbara Hancock's writing."

"No . . . I didn't. Didn't have to. Not only is Barbara married to my cousin. She is also my next-door neighbor. Has been for six years. I know her writing. Sam, Barbara did not write that letter." She studied him closely. "All right. If you prefer to doubt my judgment, I'll arrange to get a copy of her handwriting tomorrow and you can compare it yourself."

He said nothing.

"However," she said, "I thought it would have been clear to you from the beginning. Barbara couldn't have written that note."

"How is that?"

"Let's not kid ourselves. My cousin married a tramp. She was a tramp when Wilbur married her, and she kept that reputation through six years of marriage. I know that. I'm sure you know it, too. All right? Well, whoever wrote that note agreed to meet Larry Prentice in one of the drinking lounges. Let's face it. Larry might meet a woman like her on a dark corner or up a back road someplace, but *he wouldn't be caught dead with her in a public place!*"

Sure! That's what had bothered Sam about the note. The fact that the woman who wrote it had agreed to meet Prentice in public like that.

"There's a possible explanation, Justine. Maybe it wasn't a *local* lounge. Maybe it was an out-of-town lounge where nobody would recognize them."

She frowned.

"You drove Barbara to the bus Thursday. Do you know where she bought a ticket to? Supposing she just bought a ticket to Bristow and then Prentice went—"

"Sam!" She was angry. "Are you calling me a liar? Won't you accept my word for it that Barbara did *not* write that note?"

"Sorry," he said. "I had been so damned sure she had written it . . . I was thinking out loud and I guess my thinking got confused." He forced a grin. "Maybe I'm overworked. One of these days I'm going to ask my boss for a holiday."

The phone on her desk rang.

She answered it, listened, glanced narrowly at Sam, then said into the phone, "All right. I'll be in front of the office."

She hung up, stood up, retrieved her purse from her desk. "I'll be gone for two or three minutes."

He waited, listening as the door to the outer office closed. He moved silently to the outer office and watched her pass through the lobby and out onto the street.

Quickly he went to the lavatory adjoining her office. The small window looking out onto the street was set high in the wall and he was forced to stand on the toilet bowl to see out.

Wilbur Hancock's car drew to the curb. Justine hastened over and leaned in at the open car window. Darkness was settling in and Sam couldn't make out who was driving the car.

He didn't wait around in hopes of finding out.

He left the lavatory and went directly to the drawer containing the evidence. He located the note they had discovered in Prentice's pocket. It was still encased between the two sheets of glass.

> *Darling,*
> *I'll meet you in the lounge at about 5 P.M. I'll*
> *think of some excuse. Please don't forget me.*
>   *B*

He reached into his pocket and retrieved the note he had borrowed from Barbara Hancock's recipe drawer. He frowned, compared the two notes again. No, there could be no doubt. These two notes had *not* been written by the same person.

He returned the glass-encased note to the drawer, crossed to Justine's desk and poured himself another drink.

Justine's footsteps clicked determinedly across the floor of the outer office. She opened the door and strode to her desk without glancing at him. She lit a cigarette. Her hand trembled.

"That was Wilbur out there." She took a drag of her cigarette, then stubbed it and broke it into the ashtray. A tendril of red hair had escaped and hung over her forehead. She brushed it aside with the palm of her hand. "Did you deliberately let the air out of his tires and then pick him up so you could question him?"

"I didn't question him much. He said you had already talked to him so I let it go at that."

She was not mollified. "You obviously have your own ideas about Larry Prentice's death. Perhaps you don't agree with the way I'm running this office. But the fact is—I *am* running it. Perhaps after the next election you'll have your chance. That remains to be seen. But right now I'm running it, and it will be run the way *I* see fit.

"You have always been given a lot of authority from this office —both from my dad and from myself. But I want you to leave Wilbur alone. That was a childish, stupid and thoughtless thing you did, letting the air out of his tires like that and virtually *forcing* him to ride with you so you could question him. Regardless of what you may think of Wilbur, he is a very sensitive man, and I fear for what might happen. Remember, he has already attempted suicide once. They should have detained. . . . If our investigation shows that he should be questioned further, then *I* will do the questioning. Do I make myself clear on that?"

"That's pretty clear," Sam said.

She blinked her eyes as though startled by the harsh words she had just heard herself saying. She looked at him and he looked at her. It was not a contest of wills. Nor anger. It was suddenly two people attempting to recover a link of close communication that somewhere along the line had become lost.

She stood up and held out her hand. "Friends?" she said.

But he did not accept her hand. He walked around the desk and took her into his arms. For one brief moment she resisted; then all resistance was gone and she caved in against him and allowed him to kiss her lips. For a moment all barriers were down; nothing stood between them. Like old times.

"So many things, Sam," she said. "Poor little Bobby. God *damn* that Barbara!"

5

Someone entered the building. Footsteps sounded in the reception area, approached the outer office.

Sam quickly stepped away from Justine, toward his chair, as she attempted to conceal the whiskey bottle beneath her desk. There was the sound of glass hitting glass, followed by the tell-tale gurgle of escaping liquid. She reached down and the gurgling stopped.

Before she could reseat herself properly the door opened—without benefit of a knock—and Conrad Sumner appeared. He was a tall, thin, pale man. A pencil-line mustache emphasized the tight, straight line of his lips.

He strode to her desk, laid down an open envelope. "The medical examiner's report."

Sam said, "You took a fair while getting it here, Connie."

"I'm not an errand boy."

"Then why did you go out of your way to pick it up? Why not leave it to get here through the normal channels?"

Sumner ignored him, turned to Justine. "I assume you have been apprised of Blainsworth's findings?"

"Yes."

"You haven't issued any statement, I hope."

"Of course not."

"Has that newscaster, Kleinfeld, been in contact with you?"

"Yes."

"What did you tell him?"

"Absolutely nothing."

"I think he senses something—that Larry's death wasn't an accident."

"Why should he?" Sam put in. "Prentice was in three previous accidents."

"I don't know why. I'm merely stating a hunch."

He leaned toward Justine. "We've got to handle this with the utmost prudence. A scandal could be disastrous for . . . well, the entire community. We issue no statements, Justine, until we know exactly where we stand. Your office must operate in such a manner as to arouse absolutely no suspicion that Larry's death was anything other than an accident. Do you understand?"

"I'm sure we do, Conrad."

"I'll use the influence of my office to pull Blainsworth into line."

"And that would be a mistake," Sam interjected.

"I beg your pardon?"

"Doc Blainsworth will cooperate. He's apprised, as you call it, of what's at stake. He doesn't want scandal in this town any more than you want to displease the Prentices—"

"Now just a minute there!"

"And Doc will cooperate. But he won't be *pulled.* You try to *pull* him into line and he'll *pull* the rug right out from under you."

Sumner was mad and showed it. "I don't like that nasty inference that Hector Prentice will receive any more preferential consideration from my office than would any other citizen of this community."

Sam looked up at him with a scarcely veiled expression of disdain.

Sumner turned to Justine. "I'll need to be kept up to date on the developments at all times. In case there should arise any indication of a scandal, I think my judgment and legal experience should be used to the fullest."

"I'm not quite sure what you are suggesting," Justine said.

"I think my meaning is clear enough. We do everything in our power to avoid scandal."

"Well, you're going to have a scandal," Sam assured him. "Prentice was sleeping with somebody's woman when he was killed."

Sumner stiffened. "Justine, is *he* serious?"

She hesitated, then—reluctantly—nodded.

"You have proof of this?"

"We have indications."

"Do you have any idea who it might be?"

Sam looked at Justine. But she was staring at the top of her desk and shaking her head.

Sumner leaned far over Justine's desk. "Let me see these 'indications' you speak of."

"Connie," Sam said, "it's going to keep you busy running your office without trying to run this one, too."

"Justine, may I see those items." It was expressed as a command, not a question.

She glanced uncertainly toward Sam.

He said, "Sorry, Connie. We've already sent them to the lab in L.A. for analysis."

"Already!"

"We don't waste any time around here."

Sumner leaned over Justine's desk and looked her squarely in the eyes. "Have those items been sent to L.A.?"

Sam quickly stood up. "Don't you hear good?"

"Well, Justine?" Sumner demanded.

Sam placed a heavy hand on Sumner's shoulder. Sumner hit it away angrily.

"Before you hit that hand again, Connie . . . If you had tried talking to Sandy Marshal the way you're talking to his daughter, or if you had had the presumption to take a medical examiner's report before Sandy had seen it, he would have put you right through that damned window. Now why don't you let us get on with our work?"

"Don't try to intimidate me, Powell. It won't work." He turned and with great dignity walked to the door. "By the way," he stated, "the smell of raw liquor in this office is revolting."

The door closed firmly.

Justine's eyes met Sam's squarely, candidly. "Why did we lie to him about the evidence being sent to L.A.?"

"Why?"

"Why."

He decided to make his stand on this damned clear.

"I'll tell you why, Justine. Every trick in the book is going to be used to keep scandal from falling on the Prentice name. If Sumner were to discover that Larry's wallet isn't in that drawer with the rest of his stuff he'd jump on it like a cat. And Pepe Poirier would be all the excuse he would need. . . . No," he added pointedly, "I have no intention of standing by and allowing Pepe to be used as the sacrificial goat in this thing."

"How can you be so certain Pepe isn't implicated?"

"A dozen reasons. I'll give you two. Pepe is a thief. Not a robber. He would never go into Prentice's cottage with Prentice in there. On top of that, whoever choked Prentice completely collapsed his windpipe. Hell, Prentice had Pepe outweighted by thirty pounds."

"But you still don't know where Pepe got the six hundred and fifty dollars."

"No," he agreed. "I don't know where he got the six hundred and fifty dollars."

6

Justine stood up.

"Excuse me." She walked rigidly into the small lavatory.

Sam felt grubby and sticky. He had been in his clothes for over forty hours. And he suddenly realized he hadn't eaten all day.

He circled the desk and retrieved the bottle of whiskey Justine had hidden and received quite a surprise. There were *two* bottles of whiskey; the one he had brought, and another. And there was a large puddle where one of the bottles had spilled.

The lavatory door opened.

"So now you know," she said. "Really, it's not as bad as it looks. I happened to have the bottle in the car. I brought it in to have a drink. *One* drink. Is it against the law?"

He grinned to relieve the tension. "Have you taken the trouble to eat today?" he asked.

She shook her head.

"Then I've got an idea. I'll go bathe and change and come back and we'll both go out for a steak."

"You're worried maybe I'm going to sit here in the office and get stinko."

"I think we could both use a steak."

She smiled. It was a weak smile, but better than he had seen in a long time. "Sounds like fun," she said.

7

The corner of the eye is very sensitive to movement.

As Sam left the Civic Building and approached his car, he became aware of the motion across the street. Shadow within shadow. The movement was swift and furtive, and because Sam was a cop it naturally aroused his suspicions.

But he gave no indication. He leisurely crawled into his car. However, once inside he quickly swiveled his spotlight into position and snapped it on, bathing the opposite side of the street in white light.

Nobody.

Grabbing his flashlight, he ran across to where he had seen the movement—a narrow passage between the medical building and the dental clinic. No movement in the passage. He listened. There was sound all right. Retreating footsteps somewhere back there in the alley. He ran to the alley, stopped. The footsteps were headed north. He flashed his light in that direction, but the distance was too great—although he could pick out a vague indication of movement. There was a parking lot in that direction, toward the end of the block. Assuming the figure was heading for the parking lot, Sam turned off his flashlight and ran in full pursuit. Not until he was almost to the parking area did he stop and listen.

No sound at all.

Leaving his flashlight off, he moved cautiously toward the lot. Metal reflected in outline from a distant streetlight. Three cars. Maybe he had lost his man. It was easily done in a dark alley. The thing to do now was to take down the license numbers of these cars, determine who owned them and ... As he approached the first car—taking a notebook and pencil from his shirt pocket—a motor burst into life and twin Hollywood mufflers blasted the silent night air. The sound had come from half a block away. He speculated upon the possibility that the person he had been chasing might possibly have ...

The roaring mufflers must have drowned out the sound of the footsteps behind him.

When he regained consciousness he was lying where he had fallen—near the rear of the first car in the parking lot. He had been struck behind the right ear. A bad place to be hit on the head. There was a fairly large bump there, but his head didn't ache the way he felt it should. It was sore—sore as hell—but not that dull throbbing ache that should accompany a blow like that. And he wondered whether this was good or bad.

He stood up and braced himself against the car until the dizziness subsided. He didn't know offhand how long he had been unconscious. But there were now only two cars in the lot. The one that had been parked farthest from him was gone.

He flashed the light on his watch. He couldn't have been out more than three or four minutes.

His head had cleared considerably by the time he reached the Civic Building. He tried the door. It was not locked. He pushed the button to activate the night lock, then went in.

The door to Justine's outer office was open. He passed through, opened the door to her private office without knocking. She was in the process of dialing a number. His unexpected appearance caused her to stop dialing. She replaced the receiver in the cradle.

"Make a pact with you," she said thickly. "I'll knock before going into your office. You do the same here."

He was taken aback. Not so much by the near-anger in her voice as by the thick-slurry manner in which she enunciated her words. It was as though the liquor had taken a sudden and unexpected hold on her.

"I wanted to let you know I've activated the night lock on the front door. There was somebody skulking in the shadows across the street. I don't know what it means, but when I went over he ran away."

He had intended to leave it at that. But he could see that she wasn't particularly impressed by what he had said. And that could be a mistake. So he leaned over her desk and turned his head to the side. "What do you think of that little nest egg?"

"My God, Sam! Where on earth . . . ? You're not saying that whoever was over there did *that!*"

"Got me from behind."

"But why on earth . . . ? You don't suppose it was one of Pepe's friends?"

"I don't know what to make of it."

"I'd better get somebody over here to baby-sit this place while we're out for steaks."

Sam turned to leave.

"And what about after midnight?" she asked. "Have you got somebody lined up?"

"Yes."

"Who?"

"Me."

"But you haven't had a decent night's sleep since—when?"

"I can bunk down in my office as well as anyplace."

She didn't argue the point, so he turned and left. His footsteps echoed loudly through the silent building.

8

Driving back to the boarding house where he kept a room, he removed all thought of the prowler from his mind and focused his attention on Justine and that note they had found in Prentice's pocket, trying to convince himself that she wouldn't deliberately alter the evidence by substituting a phoney note. Even Sandy Marshal—probably as unorthodox a lawman as ever wore a badge—it was doubtful that even Sandy would try a stunt like that.

This office has got compassion, Sammy. Compassion. Sandy Marshal.

How much had Justine been influenced by those celebrated words?

He found his thoughts wandering into wisps of nothing. He blinked his eyes to keep them focused on the street ahead. He was obviously fatigued from lack of proper sleep.

Damn it! Damn it anyway, he thought. He swung the wheel sharply at the next corner and headed for Billy Badger's. Billy

lived above the photo studio in a weirdly decorated apartment
with an overdose of leather comfort-components and cubism
art. The shag rug on the floor was so deep it seemed to impede
the movement of the door as Billy opened it.

He was about thirty and single. He had a round face that
betrayed a slight weight problem. His eyes were an exception-
ally pale blue. He wore a vivid yellow safari shirt that hung loose
and beltless at the waist. His long hair was tousled. He did not
look to be what you would call a ladies' man. But for some
reason his glib humor and unconventional free-wheeling style
of living made him popular with any number of female tourists.
Strange how women's tastes in men changed with the times.
Was a time a woman liked her man to be—well, a man. Even
as the door opened Sam could hear soft feminine-type laughter
somewhere in the background.

"Sam?" Billy said. He belched gently and held fingers at lips
to strain the liquor fumes. He did not offer any immediate
indication that he was going to open the door wide and invite
Sam in. He gave a meaningful glance over his shoulder. "I hope
this isn't duty calling me out somewhere?"

Sam grinned, shook his head. "Wondered if you had those
pictures developed yet?"

Badger frowned. "Nobody said anything about wanting them
developed this quick. I fixed the film right away, Sam. But,
heck . . ."

"No rush. But I'd like you to project a picture of that note for
a couple of minutes. We sent the original away and I've got
something I want to compare."

Badger sighed, then grinned. "Guess that isn't going to hurt
anything very much." He told someone behind him that he
would be back shortly. Then he came out into the hall and led
Sam down a back stairway to the studio.

He placed the negative in the enlarger and focused it down
onto a piece of badly discolored plywood. The note was repro-
duced large and clear.

> *Darling,*
> *I'll meet you in the lounge at about 5 P.M. I'll*
> *think of some excuse. Please don't forget me.*
>
> *B*

Sam compared it with the note he had found in Barbara Hancock's recipe drawer, thanked Billy and left.

He felt ten feet tall. The writing was not the same. Justine had *not* substituted another note for the original. And she had been absolutely correct. Barbara Hancock had not written the note they had found in Prentice's pocket.

Back at the boarding house, under the cold shower, he considered what Justine had said about Prentice's not being "caught dead" in public with Barbara Hancock. Whoever had written this note hadn't even mentioned the name of the lounge. Which strongly indicated she had met Prentice there before—perhaps frequently.

But how could Prentice risk meeting a woman—any woman —openly in public like that?

The most logical explanation: It must be some woman Prentice was associated with through business!

He changed his clothes and replaced his big black boots with a pair of equally comfortable shoes with thick sponge-rubber soles.

9

Returning to the Civic Building to pick up Justine, he noticed there was someone in Watson's Drugstore. Kit Belman's new Mercury was parked in front. He made a U-turn and drew up behind the car. Belman was just coming from the drugstore as Sam reached the sidewalk.

"Say, Kit. Wonder if you could come down to our office tomorrow so we can write up a statement."

"Statement?"

"You were the first one at the accident. We'd like to get it on paper."

"Oh . . . certainly."

"Damned lucky you spotted that car, the way it was hidden in those trees."

"You can thank my wife for that. She noticed the reflection. You couldn't see the car at all. Obviously the sun reflecting from the roof or rear window—or something."

"And you thought it was a hubcap?"

Belman hesitated. "We were looking for the hubcap from my wife's car—yes. But when I walked back up the road to where I could see the reflection, I noticed the tire tracks going over the edge. I suspected there was something more down there than a hubcap."

Sam thanked him and watched him drive away in his big car. A Mercury for Kit, a Cadillac for Trixie. You didn't live like that on Kit's salary. Trixie's old man was obviously throwing plenty of dough into the kitty. And old Sedgewick had plenty of money to throw. Someday Belman was going to find himself on the happy side of a million bucks. Sam wondered, cynically, whether a lifetime with Trixie was really worth it all. What the hell. It takes all kinds.

The door to the drugstore was locked, but Booker was inside setting up some shelves. He let Sam in.

"Just getting things ready for the back-to-school trade," he said, wiping chalk-dust from his hands.

Booker Watson was going into his fourth term as a councilman. He was fifty-some and just beginning to show indications of too much eating and too little exercise. He had never been a handsome man, but he had a way with the public. He had a highly successful business.

"I was thinking of giving you a call, Sam. Terrible accident. How did it happen?"

"We're not sure."

Watson was a confirmed busybody. Sam would have to be careful how he handled this.

"Was he drunk?" Booker asked.

"We don't know yet, Booker," Sam lied.

"I hear it wasn't pretty."

"Accidents never are. I understand you and Larry were the silent partners in that new laundromat-carwash."

"It's not much of a secret."

"Where did he do most of his drinking?"

"I don't know anything about his private life. We happened to invest in the same business. That's as far as it went."

"How many people you got working for you down there?"

"Three."

Sam seemed surprised. "Is that all it takes to run an operation like that?"

The druggist smiled, self-satisfied. "Automation, Sam. Mind you, now that doesn't include Mrs. Kell, who runs the office."

"Mrs. Kell? That's a new name to me."

Watson nodded. "She and her husband moved here only three or four months ago."

"Is she the one they call Bonny or Bunny or Blanch or something like that?"

Watson shook his head. "Elsie."

"But hasn't she got a nickname?"

"Not that I've ever heard."

"Must have been the woman you had working there before her, then."

"No. Elsie started with us the day we opened the doors."

"Well, that's damned funny," Sam said with an attitude of deep puzzlement.

"What's funny, Sam?"

"Larry introduced me to a woman a while back. I'm sure her name started with *B.* I got the impression that she was involved in some kind of business with him. I thought it was the car-wash."

"No. Most likely it was somebody who worked in his dad's department store."

"Most likely," Sam said and returned to his car.

Booker Watson stared out the door, a quizzical expression on his face.

Sam entered the Civic Building. The pneumatic attachment on the big entrance door brought it closed very silently. There was nobody behind the front desk. The door to Justine's outer office was still open. The door to her private office was also ajar. She had obviously left it that way so she could hear him—or anyone else for that matter—as he entered the building. But the sponge-soled shoes made not a sound. He could hear her talking on the telephone. He was about to knock on the panel of her door—but stopped.

". . . I tell you there is nothing to worry about. I talked to him and I warned him to leave you alone. So please don't worry yourself. He won't bother you. . . . I know you can't. But he won't ask you any more questions. . . . Is Bobby there? . . . Oh. . . . Well, goodnight, Wilbur."

10

He stepped away from her door and quickly retreated to the lobby. He was almost to the entrance door when he heard her footsteps coming through the outer office. He spun around to make it look as though he were just entering the building and began whistling softly.

Her face was highly flushed and she looked at him almost petulantly. She seemed about to say something, but at the moment she turned her ankle and had to clutch the desk for support. "Oooops!" She attempted to smile but it was a ludicrous effort.

"Get anybody to tend the shop?" he asked.

"Sill Philvers is stopping in."

Sam winced. Bejeezus, if she wasn't tight.

He walked past her into her office. He went behind her desk to get his bottle. It was there, all right. And so was the other bottle. But the other bottle was now empty. Furthermore, she had either spilled some more of it or hadn't bothered to wipe up the puddle made earlier in the evening—which wasn't like Justine at all. Matter of fact, he had never before seen her tight. She was a plenty mixed-up girl right now.

The thing to do was get her home, have Aida put her to bed.

He picked up his bottle, approached Justine and gently touched her arm. "I think you'd better wait in my car till Phil gets here."

"Why?"

"You're tight, Justine."

"Does it show?"

"It shows."

"Wouldn't want the saff to stee."

No.

He locked her office door, placed his arm around her and walked with her out to his car. He had just got her into the car nicely when Silvers arrived. He told Silvers he would try to be back before midnight.

As he was drawing away from the curb the radio crackled and Curly Cameron came through. "I've found the Mink car."

"The what?"

"Pepe Poirier's girl friend. I found her car. It's up the lake shore road about two miles. In the trees."

"How about the girl?"

"She isn't in the car. My bloody flashlight is dead."

"I'll be right there."

Justine said, "I'm coming along."

"But do you think you're in fit—"

"I won't even get out of the car."

Titan had been built around the northeast point of Lake Titan. To get to the lake shore road you drove south out of town, past a string of garish motels. The road meandered south along the east shore of the lake. To the right were sand and rock and lake. To the left, with the exception of the odd dwelling, there were only trees, trees spreading out and up almost to the snowline.

Sam drew to a stop a good distance from Curly's cruiser. He touched Justine's shoulder and she ducked down from sight while he opened the door and the dome light went on. Curly led him to the abandoned car deep in the trees.

"In daylight I wouldn't have seen it. My spotlight picked up the reflection."

The motor was cold. The key was not in the ignition.

Sam shone his flashlight into the surrounding bushes. But there was no indication which direction she had gone.

"Hold on!" Curly exclaimed. "Back a little with the light. . . . There!" He ran into the bushes and retrieved a small metal object on a chain. "The key to the car."

And he was right.

"Looks like she just got out of the car and threw it," Curly said. "But it hit the bushes and didn't go far."

"If she threw away the key, then she didn't plan on coming back for the car."

Sam placed the key in the ignition and turned it. The gas gauge showed half full.

"It doesn't look good, Sam. This car is a powerhouse. Her natural reaction would be to use the car to get away in."

"Unless she was a real pro. Then she'd know the easiest way for us to spot her would be through the car."

"She must have been expecting real trouble or she would never have abandoned a car like this," Curly maintained.

Sam inserted the key in the lock of the trunk and was about to open it when Curly said, "Hold it, Sam. Car coming."

The car drove past them, then stopped. The door opened.

Curly muttered a soft curse. "It's Schuyler Kleinfeld, for crissake."

"Trouble, boys?" Schuyler asked.

"No trouble."

Sam moved into such a position as to obstruct Kleinfeld's view of the license plate on the abandoned car.

"What brings you way out this way this time of night, Sky?" Curly asked.

"Getting a breath of good lake air before my next newscast."

"Don't tell me you've put yourself on twenty-four-hours-a-day duty over there?"

"Only when something really big breaks," he replied enigmatically. He strolled casually to the side of the car. "Nice car." He shot the beam of his flashlight inside.

"Come on, Sky," Curly said. "You know better than to bugger around like this. If it's anything you should know about we'll let you know."

"No offense. Anything new for me on the Prentice thing?"

"We'll let you know," Sam said.

When the broadcaster had left, Curly asked, "What do you suppose he meant by 'something big breaking'? You don't suppose he's got wind that Prentice was murdered?"

"Not a chance."

Curly pushed back his hat and scratched his head thoughtfully. "Hell of a coincidence he should just happen past here like that."

"It has to be a coincidence," Sam replied. "I wasn't followed."

"That kind of a coincidence makes me worry a little, Sam."

"I'm worrying enough for both of us. Let's see what's in that trunk."

They opened the trunk. The light didn't go on. Sam used his flashlight. At first glance everything appeared perfectly normal. There were a jack and a spare tire. Sam pushed the tire with his thumb. There was no air in it. He lifted it up and shook it. Nothing loose inside.

"Phone Wollinski's," he said. "Have them tow this thing up to their place. Tomorrow I want you to go over this car with a fine-tooth comb."

He dumped the tire back into the trunk.

"Hold it, Sam," Curly cried. "Shine the light back in there again.... Look! What the hell do you make of *those little things?*"

Small black particles were scattered across the bottom of the trunk. They were very fine and almost indistinguishable against the rubberized fabric.

Sam picked up some of them in his fingers. They had a rubbery texture. Like rubber filings.

"Oh, oh," Sam exclaimed, picking up the spare tire again and turning it over. "There's your answer," he said, indicating where someone had sawed a hole about three inches square in the tire.

"Looks like whatever we might have found is gone," Curly said.

Sam walked to Curly's cruiser and picked up the mobile telephone. "It's a pretty late hour, but doggone it, I'm going to call Herman Munsterburg and see if we can get him over here with that dog of his."

He made contact with the Munsterburg farm and got the man out of bed. But Munsterburg was always affable, and when he learned they wanted to use his dog for police work he was all enthusiasm.

"He'll be right over," Sam told Curly.

"What are you hoping the dog will turn up?" Curly asked. "Some sort of a miracle?"

"Something like that," Sam said.

11

Sam closed the trunk of the abandoned car, locked it and gave Curly the key.

"We better remove these license plates and any identification that might be in the car. Just in case Kleinfeld comes back snooping around here."

Curly placed a cigarette in his mouth and looked at Sam thoughtfully in the light of the match. "Prentice's wallet is missing, and Pepe Poirier has got a lot of money he can't account for. You've never suggested there might be a connection, and I can't help but wonder why."

"I haven't mentioned it because a rumor like that might give Hector Prentice the wrong idea, and it could bring us a lot of trouble."

"Then you don't think there is a connection?"

"No, I don't."

"That's got to be more than a hunch."

"It is," Sam said laconically and began undoing a wingnut on the rear license.

Curly waited a moment, but Sam obviously didn't consider it necessary to elucidate further on the subject, so Curly proceeded around to the front license plate.

"Silent" Sam. It was a nickname Sandy Marshal had given Sam years ago because of this provoking habit of keeping his ideas to himself. Deputies often found themselves working assignments without knowing why. Nobody particularly liked this lack of communication, but mostly they learned to live with it.

A few minutes later Curly was seated in his cruiser. Sam joined him and held up a pair of slender feminine stockings. "Think these'll do?" he asked.

Curly studied them in the light from the dash, a broad smile spreading across his face. "So you do have your moments." He pinched Sam good-naturedly on the thigh. "Don't tell me your friend is sitting over there with her clothes off."

Sam glanced toward his cruiser. You couldn't make out Justine's features at all. But the cigarette she was smoking stood out like a small red beacon.

"You've got the wrong idea," he said. "I got these stockings from the glove compartment of the Mink girl's car. We'll have to have something with her scent on it so the dog will know what trail to follow. I'm hoping these are her stockings."

"I imagine they are." But Curly sounded disappointed. "Damn it, you had me real excited there for a minute. By the way, who *is* your friend?"

"You wouldn't know her," Sam said.

Munsterburg arrived in his car. Sam hastened over to meet him. He reached out to open the door for Herman but changed his mind fast and stepped back. The rear window was open. A deadly growl had erupted from within, and a dog's head appeared, baring its teeth viciously. This was Fritz, Munsterburg's beautiful black and tan German shepherd. He weighed close to a hundred pounds and he had been trained to protect this car. Sam knew the dog well and had no doubt that his bite was a hell of a lot worse than his bark.

Munsterburg glanced back at his pet, said, "Free," and the dog leaped through the window, missing Sam by no more than a foot.

Once out of the car and off command, the dog came over to Sam and nuzzled up to him. Sam patted him on the head. They were friends of long standing.

Munsterburg wasted no time putting his highly trained animal into action. He led him over to the driver's side of the car. Taking one of the Mink girl's stockings, he held it to the dog's nose. "Fritz. *Such!*" he said. *"Such!"* And as he uttered the command, he lowered the stocking to the ground approximately where the girl must have stepped down when leaving the car. Having done this, he stepped back and let the dog go to work.

This was the same dog that had gained wide acclaim two years earlier when he had discovered the bodies of England's vacationing finance minister and his secretary beneath ten feet of snow on Mt. Titan. He knew his business and it was a thrill to watch him in action.

He picked up the scent quickly and—nose close to the ground —followed it to the rear of the car where the girl must have stood when she was sawing the tire. He circled the car, returning to where he had started. Holding his head high, he moved directly to the spot from which Curly had retrieved the key.

"Son of a gun!" Curly exclaimed softly.

The dog seemed confused now. He returned to the car. He struck out in a wide zigzag course. He was obviously not following a scent but trying to find one.

"How old is this track?" Munsterburg asked.

"Could be as much as twenty-four hours."

"We see," the farmer said. "We see." He sounded singularly optimistic.

He knew his dog. The animal came to a dead stop, turned, went back about two feet, and seemed almost to dig its muzzle into the earth; then, nose only an inch or two above the ground, it started off through the trees.

The three men followed, Munsterburg in the lead. He kept his light beamed on the dog. The dog stopped and began digging.

"He's found something," Munsterburg said.

"*Don't* let him dig, Herman!" Sam said.

"Fritz!" Munsterburg cried. *"Nein! Nein!"* The dog stopped digging. *"Sitz!"* The dog sat down.

Sam dropped to his knees where the dog had been digging and carefully scraped back the soil with his hands. The soil was, for the most part, a damp humus of rotted leaves. His finger touched something hard. He flicked at the humus with the backs of his fingers, then blew at it. He trained his flashlight on the object he had unearthed, then quickly shielded it with his hand as Munsterburg bent over his shoulder to see what it was.

"Herman," he said, "you—uh—keep the dog following the trail. Keep at it."

"Sure, Sam." And the farmer once again put his dog to work.

A motor roared into life. The unexpected sound issued from the direction of the abandoned car.

"What the devil is going on back there?" Curly said.

"You better check it fast," Sam said.

Curly, without benefit of a flashlight, made his way noisily through the trees. Three minutes later he was back.

"Whoever that friend of yours *was*, Sam—she drove off in your cruiser."

"Don't worry about the car," Sam said. "Let's go and see how Munsterburg and his dog are making out."

"Hold on! *Just* a shake now." Curly walked over to where Sam had been digging in the ground. But there was no longer any indication that he had been digging. Dead leaves covered the spot. The earth looked undisturbed. "Let's have it, Sam. What did you find there?"

"Later."

"Later nothing. I've got a right to know what you found. Doggone it, I want to know."

"For your own peace of mind, Curly, just let it lie. Give me one day, maybe two—then I'll show you."

"No dice."

"Munsterburg is coming."

"Show it to me."

Sam obviously didn't like Curly's attitude, and Curly obviously didn't give a damn whether Sam liked it or not.

Reluctantly Sam reached into his pocket and brought out his carefully folded handkerchief. Unwrapping it, he took hold of an object by the corners and drew it upward. It unfolded like an accordion, displaying to full view four credit cards. They were enclosed in a plastic window-stripping of the type that folds compactly into a wallet. The jagged edges at one end of the plastic strip indicated that it had been ripped from a wallet. Three of the cards had been issued by oil companies, the fourth by a prominent men's wear store in Los Angeles.

Indented into each card was the name: L. R. Prentice.

12

Conrad Sumner had struck gold.

He unlocked the entrance door of the Civic Building, strode past Phil Silvers at the front desk and proceeded directly to the sheriff's office.

"Nobody in there," Silvers told him.

Sumner whirled. "Where is she?"

"Don't know."

"Her mother said she was here."

"Well, she isn't."

"How about Powell? Where's he?"

"Steak Loft having supper."

"At this ridiculous hour?"

"We don't have regular hours on this job." His voice indicated little in the way of respect. Sumner made a mental note of this fact.

He went directly to his office down the corridor and phoned the Loft. Powell was not there. Sumner looked up the number of his cruiser and dialed it. The voice at the other end surprised him.

"Justine Marshal speaking."

"Sheriff, this is Conrad Sumner. I'm glad I finally contacted you. I have a question for you to answer."

"Yes . . . ?"

"How much money was on Larry Prentice's person when you found him?"

There was a pause. As it drew out, a grin twisted at Sumner's mouth.

"Where are you calling from?" she asked.

"I hardly see how that is pertinent to the question."

"Are you at the Civic Building?"

"I am. In my office."

"I'll be there shortly."

"Yes," he said. "By all means."

She stepped into his office less than ten minutes later. Her face was flushed, her eyes slightly dilated. Quite obvious indications of alcohol. And he recalled the strong odor of alcohol he had detected in her office earlier that evening. He reflected upon what she might have been doing in Powell's cruiser at this late hour. It was rather common knowledge there had been something going on between these two several years ago. However, he had been under the distinct impression that their relationship had been rather strained since her return to Titan. Nevertheless, he was surprised to find she was alone. She had been in Powell's car. Yet Powell hadn't accompanied her. Strange. . . . Running interference for this beautiful sheriff had seemed, of late, to be Powell's self-appointed mission in life.

He watched her as she found a straight-backed chair and sat down. Still wearing those jodhpurs and riding boots. And that checkered man's shirt. Was it her contention that by dressing like a man, she could fill a man's shoes? If only she understood the psychological connotations of a woman who wore riding attire when there was no horse to ride. Really, she was quite transparent, this sadistic pretender.

He sat behind his desk and stared at her, tapping his pencil impatiently, waiting for her to answer the question he had placed to her over the telephone. He had no intention of making this confrontation easy for her.

She fidgeted, cleared her throat, brushed a hank of hair away from her right eye. "You were asking about Larry Prentice's money?"

He continued to stare at her, not speaking, allowing her to stew.

"There was no money, Conrad."

"None at *all?* You mean the wallet was *empty?*"

"There was no wallet."

Beautiful. Beautiful. Everything was fitting so beautifully.

"Did you know that Larry Prentice left town Thursday on a business trip?" he demanded.

"Yes."

"And were you aware of the fact that before leaving he withdrew from the bank"—he glanced at a paper on his desk—"six hundred and eighty dollars?"

"No. We didn't have that information."

"And according to this information from your office"—he held up a familiar rectangular memo sheet—"six hundred and fifty dollars was found in the bed leg in Pepe Poirier's hotel room. Money for which Poirier cannot account. Considering that Poirier is virtually an habitual criminal—a thief—aren't these various pieces of information beginning to tell you a story, sheriff?"

"A story of circumstances, Conrad. Certainly nothing indictable. Not at this point. You'll have all the facts when we have completed our investigation."

"In the meantime I would like an itemized list of the evidence you have compiled concerning Larry's death."

"You'll have one on your desk tomorrow morning."

"And right now," he said, "I would like to see the money you found in Poirier's possession."

"Why?"

"Shall we say I'm curious?"

"Do you have the numbers of the bills Larry withdrew from the bank? Is that what you're saying?"

"Not at all."

"What are you saying?"

"I'm saying that I would like to see that money."

"Damn it, Conrad! If you have information pertinent to this case it's only proper it should be passed on to the sheriff's office."

"Sheriff," he said, "when I have the proper information—you'll hear about it. Make no mistake about that."

13

The night was black and very still.

The lake lay like a giant sounding board. A steam whistle sounded in the far distance. One of the old freight trains hauling coal from the mines, headed eventually to the Pacific coast, then ultimately by boat to Japan. It was a good sound, the sound of that old steam whistle. There was a time when it had almost disappeared from the valley as, one by one, the industrial giants of North America decided that coal was no longer an economical source of energy. The Titan Valley coal industry had gone into a real slump. Then came the fabulous Japanese contract—coal to infinitude! And Sam often wondered how it was that Japan could afford to import this coal all the way across the Pacific Ocean, use it to manufacture its goods, export those goods all the way back across the Pacific again, and still sell them for less money than the stuff made right here at home. A real puzzle. But at this moment he had other thoughts on his mind than the mysteries of the aggressive Japanese economy.

"How do you see it, Sam?" Curly asked.

Munsterburg's dog had followed the Mink girl's scent back to the road but had been unable to trace it beyond that. Apparently she had been picked up by an automobile. Munsterburg had gone home to bed, and Wollinski had towed away the abandoned car. Curly and Sam were standing beside Curly's cruiser having a smoke.

"How do you see it, Sam?" Curly asked.

"I'm hoping that when I dangle those credit cards in front of Pepe's nose he'll smarten up and tell us how he came to get them. Or how the girl came to get them. And the money."

"Personally, Sam"—Curly's voice was gentle—"I think those credit cards say everything that has to be said."

Sam looked at him, and the glow from his cigarette was bright enough to disclose the frown. "Curly, *you* don't think Pepe killed Prentice?"

"I know how you feel, Sam. I don't blame you. Hell, you gave that guy every break in the—"

"That has nothing to do with it," Sam said. "It just doesn't fit right to be Pepe. None of it." He walked around and got into the cruiser.

Curly slid in behind the wheel, turned on the dome light. The credit cards were on the seat between them, wrapped in Sam's handkerchief. "Tell me why you don't think it was Pepe's work, Sam."

"The most obvious reason is that Pepe doesn't have any scratches on him. We know that Prentice scratched his killer."

"Or we're led to believe he did," Curly said. "It can be rigged. You know that. We don't know where that skin under Prentice's nails actually came from. And it might have been the Mink girl Prentice scratched. The scratches didn't necessarily have to be on her face, Sam. And she sure as hell isn't around here to disprove it.

"Personally," he continued, "I think she ran because she *knew* Prentice was dead. . . . There's just no other way it makes sense. She knew he was dead, because she was there when he got killed. I'm saying she was the one Prentice was laying when he got killed."

Sam gave him a strange look and Curly said, "Don't look so shocked. Just think back a few years. Remember that old 'under-the-bed' trick and that wild little Hershel bitch who used to live here? Remember her?"

"I remember her."

"She and Pepe used to work the trick together. Hell, they were only kids. She used to lure married travelers from out of town into her house when her dad was working nights in the mine. Pepe would be under the bed. The traveler would undress and naturally lay his clothes beside the bed. When the action began Pepe would take the money out of the guy's clothes, crawl out of the room and then knock on the front door. Then the girl would say, 'Oh, goodness, I think it's the police again.' The poor bloody traveler would panic, grab his clothes and clear the hell out of there fast. By the time he found the money gone it was too late. Remember?"

"I remember the stunt."

"It was damned near foolproof. There aren't many men who would bring charges and face the consequences of being shacked up with a fifteen-year-old kid.

"Well, to make my point, I think Pepe and this whore Delores Mink planned to work the same principle on Prentice. Only it being Prentice's cabin, it would be the girl who went out the back way. Prentice would go to answer the knock on the door, there'd be nobody there, and when he got back to the bedroom the girl would be gone, too. They figured he wouldn't dare put in a complaint, because it would mean admitting he had been shacked up with a whore.

"Only the trouble was, they didn't know Prentice like we do. He might be a whoremaster, but he's a pernickety whoremaster. Prentice wouldn't throw his clothes on the floor like the average guy. It's his cottage, so the natural thing for a guy like him to do is to hang his clothes in the closet.

"This complicates things, and when Pepe tries to get the money out of the closet Prentice spots him. Pepe panics, this panic gives him strength he wouldn't normally have, and he chokes Prentice to death. . . . Well?"

Sam shifted his position, scratched thoughtfully at his crotch. "You didn't dream up a theory like that on the spur of the moment."

Curly nodded. "Particularly when I found the Mink girl had left this car behind. To me it could only mean she knew ahead of time that Prentice was dead."

Sam reflected on it for a while. "Connie Sumner could make a good case out of it."

"Flight is an admission of guilt. Hell, Sam, I don't think there's a doubt, the way things stand right now, Connie could get himself a conviction."

He started the motor and they headed back toward town.

14

The speaker crackled on the two-way. "Home to car Cameron. Home to car Cameron." It was Justine.

"I'll take it," Sam said. He picked up the microphone and activated the thumb switch. "Go ahead, Justine. Curly and I are on our way back to the office."

"Just had a call from a Mrs. Dibbs at Thirty-nine Belton. She suspects mischief over there."

"What sort of mischief?"

"You two boys go over there and talk to her," she replied evasively.

There was the influence again of that three-year trick she had served with the L.A. police department. She never liked to put things into their proper words when she was talking on the two-way. She had even suggested they adopt those number codes like they used in the cities. Sam considered it unnecessary. He reminded her that her dad also had considered it unnecessary and a waste of time. So she had let the idea drop.

"We're on our way," Sam said.

It wasn't hard to spot 39 Belton. Every light in the house was on, including the porch light and a small spotlight which had been set on the front lawn for the purpose of illuminating a large, beautifully cultured rock garden but was now swung around and positioned so as to shine right in your face as you passed through the entrance in the hedges at the front of the house.

Curly and Sam entered the hedge-fronted yard and blinked against the blinding glare. The forty-foot walk leading to the house was bordered on either side by a profusion of beautiful flowers. They were halfway up the walk when the front door flew open and a woman charged out, extending her open arms to them in a frantic show of welcome.

She was a tall woman, about sixty years old and thin as a rake. Sam recognized her immediately as the woman Oscar Quibell frequently referred to as "Rebecca Dibbs, the flower lady." She periodically presented Oscar with bouquets of flowers to bring down to the Civic Building and brighten up those "dingy offices."

"Thank goodness you're here!" she cried. "Thank goodness!" Her voice had an unusual crackling break to it as though in sixty-odd years it hadn't yet quite decided whether to remain soprano or become contralto.

"What's the problem, Mrs. Dibbs?"

She caught her breath, stared at Sam's hip, then at Curly's. "Where are your guns?"

"Figure we need guns?"

She nodded vigorously, stared off into the darkness to her left. In a suddenly hushed voice, "I saw somebody being beaten. Hit over the head. Maybe *killed!*"

Sam glanced into the darkness where the light from the spotlight didn't reach.

"Not over there—out *there!* On the street—on the sidewalk. Up there. Up by—*Oscar's!*"

"Oscar's?"

"Oscar! You know Oscar. Oscar *Quibell!* Good heavens, he tends the Civic Building—"

"This happened on the sidewalk outside Oscar's house, eh?"

"Yes. *About* that. I can't say it was *exactly* there. But up that way."

"How far is Oscar's from here?"

"You know where Oscar lives."

"Is it two houses or three houses?"

"Three."

Sam handed Curly his flashlight and Curly asked Mrs. Dibbs, "Did it happen right out on the sidewalk?"

"Yes."

Curly disappeared.

"*When* did this happen?" Sam asked.

"Oh—time goes so funny at a time like this. Let's see. It's—what?—*ten* after *twelve!* After midnight *already?* I had no idea. Time just—well, seems to disappear. I was so scared, so—you know?"

"I sure do, Mrs. Dibbs."

"Let me see now—"

The cruiser door slammed. Sam could hear Curly's footsteps as he left the cruiser and moved up the sidewalk toward where Mrs. Dibbs had seen somebody being "killed."

"*Marcus Welby* ended at eleven. I watched the local news, then somebody in Los Angeles or someplace started interviewing one of those Black Panthers or whatever you call them. Seems you can't turn the set on these days but they're talking about those race riots and like that. Heavens, we never have that problem here in Titan. I just don't understand those people out there. There's an East Indian dentist moved in down the street a few weeks ago and we treat him just like he was one of us— Aren't you going to check out there and see what happened?"

"My partner is checking. I'm interested in when it happened, Rebecca."

"You know my name." A smile crossed her austere face. "You've heard Oscar speak of me."

"We've appreciated those flowers you sent us. You were saying you watched the local news, and then . . . ?"

"Well, I didn't want to watch that other thing so I decided to come and smell the flowers. I was wearing my bedroom slippers. Thank goodness. Or he might have heard me. I knew the breeze was blowing from the lake. When it's from that direction you can smell my rockery clear out onto the street. My rock garden. You can't see it very clear with that spotlight turned away from it, but it's—well, it's quite lovely. Only this year it was hit by that late frost. Anyway, like I say, I was in my bedroom slippers and I walked out as far as the entrance gate there where you folks came in through. I was standing there, what you might say right in the hedges. I hadn't been there more than five minutes. And that's when I heard the sound of the man getting killed."

"What sort of a sound was it, Rebecca?"

"I'm trying to remember. And keep all these facts clear in my mind. It isn't easy, you know—so unexpected and all. Well . . . I would recall it as being a yell, and then a sort of choking sound."

"A real loud yell?"

"No. But loud enough for me to hear. And then some. The choking wasn't so loud. I stuck my head out past the hedges. That's when I saw him hit him over the head with the bar or whatever it was."

"You say this happened down about where Oscar lives?"

"Yes."

"Did you recognize either of the men?"

"No."

"What do you remember about them?"

"I remember that bar coming down on the other man's head."

"Were they large men, do you think?"

"I'm trying to remember. I don't want to say anything that will mix you up. I saw one time on *Ironsides*—you ever watch *Ironsides?* It's that one with Raymond Burr and that nigger and —you must know *Ironsides?*"

"Sure."

"Well, I saw on there one time where they proved that most of what witnesses think they saw isn't what they saw at all. So I'm trying not to make that mistake. And to be honest about it, I don't know whether they were big men or not. I'm sorry."

"What did you do when you saw the man being hit?"

"I . . . just don't remember. I don't even remember turning that spotlight around so's it would shine over there on the gate like that. But I must have."

"Were all these lights on when this happened?"

"Lord no. I wouldn't want the neighbors to see me out looking at my flowers that time of night. They might think I'm conceited or something. And I'm not. But you've got to be careful how you act once you start winning awards or people might get the wrong ideas. You see, my yard won the Prentice award four years ago, and I received honorable mention for my rockery the last two years in a row. Except this year, of course, what with that frost. . . . But I guess you know that."

"Beautiful yard," Sam said.

"Thank you. But it isn't anything to what it usually is."

"So none of these lights were on?"

"No. The only light that was on in the whole house was that little fifteen-watt lamp I keep on over the TV so's it won't strain my eyes."

Sam glanced around. They had arrived here without using the siren, and, so near as he could judge, neither Becky's bright lights nor the arrival of the cruiser had caused any undue attention. Virtually all the houses were in darkness.

"Where is the switch for the spotlight, Rebecca?"

"Right inside the front door."

"Maybe you should turn it off now."

She did that, then returned to where he was standing just beyond the illumination of the porch light.

"You must have called the sheriff's office about midnight. You have no idea what you did in that thirty-five or forty minutes between the time you heard the choking sound and the time you made the call?"

"I know I stood there in the darkness of the house for a long time. I didn't realize it was near that long, though. Time's funny. Then I turned on all the lights and I phoned Oscar at his house. But he must have already left for work, because I didn't get an answer. Then when I phoned down there the sheriff answered."

Footsteps. Curly came into the yard. He was wearing his holstered .38 Police Special clipped to his belt. As he approached he turned off the flashlight.

"Well?" she asked.

"You're sure this happened right on the sidewalk, Mrs. Dibbs?"

"What . . . ? You mean you couldn't find him . . . or . . . *anything?*"

"Maybe if you show us where you think it happened? Sort of—"

"I know," she said quickly. "Re-create the scene of the crime."

"Sure," Sam said. "Just like on *Ironsides.*"

"Huh?" Curly asked. "Like on what?"

Sam ignored him and suggested to Mrs. Dibbs that "because there were no lights on when you saw it happen, maybe you should go up and turn off the porch lights."

She did. Curly flicked on his flashlight. She returned and took her position near the hedge where she had been standing when she heard the choking sound.

"I'll start walking down the street," Curly said. "You yell for me to stop when I get to about the spot where you saw it happen."

"All right."

They were situated roughly in the middle of the block. There were streetlights at either intersection, but the light was absorbed and lost in the foliage of the many trees. Without a moon it was very dark.

When Curly had progressed about twenty feet up the sidewalk he turned off his flashlight. They could hear his footsteps on the concrete as he continued along the sidewalk.

"You'll have to turn that light on again," she called. "I can't see a thing."

Curly stopped walking. But he did not turn on his light. Neither he nor Sam said a word. The silence became prolonged.

Then, "You think I'm lying!" she cried. "I saw it, I tell you. I saw it *happen!*"

Silence was the suggested procedure here. Neither deputy said a word. Neither moved. The dark silence was unnerving.

"You should know better than to treat me like this," she cried. "It's not good for my heart. Just wait till Doctor Blainsworth hears about it. I called you over here in good faith and you treat me like a . . . like a *liar!*"

"We didn't accuse you of lying, Mrs. Dibbs."

"Silence speaks louder than words. I know what you're thinking. You just wait till Doctor Blainsworth hears about this."

"Has Doc been treating you lately?"

"Yes. All the time. For my heart. He said I wasn't to get excited like this."

"And you shouldn't, Rebecca," Sam said. He spoke softly. "We're not saying you lied to us at all. Heck, maybe the moon was shining. Maybe that's how you saw him?"

"It must have been. I only know what I saw."

"Sure. No need to get excited at all. Best thing for you to do is to go back in the house and relax. *Midnight Matinée* has just started. My partner and I will look around up there real good, and then we'll come back again tomorrow and look around some more. Now don't you worry yourself, Rebecca."

"Should I lock my door?"

"Yes," Sam said. "That'll be all right. But there'll be some-body driving around here off and on all night. So don't you fret yourself."

"Thank you, Sam."

He listened to her lock the door, then rejoined Curly.

"Damn it, Sam," Curly said, "There was no moon tonight."

"No," Sam said. "It was as dark an hour ago as it is right now."

"Why should she pull a stunt like that?"

Sam thought about it. "Could be what they call compensat-ing. She's an old lady, and likely a *lonely* lady. Generally she gets attention by growing some of the nicest flowers in the valley. This year the frost hit her flowers. Maybe this is a way of making up for the attention she's not getting this year from the flowers.

"Seems sort of a coincidence it should happen on Oscar's night off and happen right down there in front of Oscar's and that the first person she called—or tried to call—was Oscar."

"I get it," Curly said. "You think she initially dreamed this up to get Oscar's attention?"

"Sure. Then, on the spur of the moment, decided to go along with the story anyway."

"Poor old dame. Having to resort to a stunt like that for attention." Curly started toward the cruiser. "Let's go have ourselves a cup of coffee somewhere."

"Did you check inside the hedges up at Oscar's?"

"And including both houses on this side and the one on the other. There's no heel marks. No nothing. No sign anybody was dragged or that anybody was hurt. I think we've humored the old dame enough. Let's go for coffee."

"Let me see the flashlight for a minute, Curly." Sam disappeared and didn't return for three or four minutes.

"Where you been?"

"Just checking to see if Oscar's car was gone. It was."

"Why did you do that?"

"I don't know why. Just going through the motions, I suppose."

"No doubt in my mind where Oscar is," Curly said. "He's up at that little shack of his on Varden Crick. That's where Oscar is."

15

They were on their way for a coffee when the two-way crackled into life. "Car Silvers to home. Car Silvers to home."

Sam waited for ten seconds. When Justine didn't come through from the office, he scooped up the microphone. "Phil, where the hell are you?"

"Down at Jake's Café. There was a report of a fight. The sheriff told me to look in on it. But it wasn't much. Two miners. They've agreed to pay for the damages. I can bring them in if you like."

"No. Get their names, then let them go. Who's back at the office?"

"Gee, I thought the sheriff was."

Justine's voice broke in. "I am. I was busy on the phone when you called through."

"Do I come back to the station now?" Phil asked.

When Justine didn't answer immediately, Sam pushed the button and said, "Call it a day, Phil. But be around sharp at eight tomorrow morning. It'll be overtime for everybody tomorrow."

He listened a moment to see if Justine had anything further to

say, then, "Looks like a false alarm over here on Belton, Justine
I'll be back to the office in about twenty minutes."

"Over and out," she said. And that was all she said.

"You know," Curly said, "maybe we should have our coffee
down there at Jake's Cafe where the fight was. Throw a scare
into that bunch who hang around down there. Let them know
the sheriff's office is really on the job."

Sam considered it, then shook his head. "Jesus, Curly. I don't
know. It might hurt Jake's business. We've got to give those
old-timers like Jake every break we can. Things are getting
tough for them."

"Yes. I suppose they are. With all those new posh places
opening up."

"Three or four years ago a man would take his wife and family
into Jake's and feel right at home about it. Now, with all the new
development, people are starting to look on Jake's and those
other places on Lake Street as a sort of a slum. Jake's hurting.
So are the rest of them. Even the Lakeside Hotel."

"Imagine Poirier moving his whore into the Lakeside. Son of
a bitch. It's a sign of the times, Sam. Everything's changing."

They had their coffee at a new twenty four-hour operation
called the Titan Spa. It featured a heated mineral-water swim-
ming pool built right into the roof, with special minerals that
were said to be imported all the way from Belgium. Somebody
had told Sam that it didn't smell so hot, but it was supposed to
draw the nicotine and other impurities right out onto your skin.
Sam and Curly didn't go up to the pool. They took a table near
a palm tree growing right out of the floor, and Sam had four
eggs and seven slices of fried ham. Curly had three cups of
coffee. The bill came to over five dollars.

"Ouch," Curly said.

Sam was waiting to pay the bill when a slender man in a silk
suit came up to him, took the bill and made an elaborate show
of ripping it in half. "I'm Findlay Winston, Mr. Powell. It's nice
to have you drop in. And it's on the house, Mr. Powell."

"A real nice gesture, Mr. Winston." Sam handed him a ten-dollar bill. "Of course we can't accept it. You understand."

Winston took the money and reluctantly rang up the sale. "Come again, sheriff."

Out in the cruiser Curly said, "Notice how he called you sheriff."

"That's supposed to make me feel good, Curly."

"How to win friends and influence people. Boy, that new bunch doesn't miss a trick. I'd a been half tempted to take the guy up on the offer. They claim Schuyler Kleinfeld never pays for anything in this town anymore. The merchants keep him stocked up, and he returns the favor by giving them free plugs on his radio and TV shows."

"Sure," Sam said. "Sky can return the favor with free plugs. But how do we return the favor?"

"See what you mean. A guy would never want to put himself in a position where he felt he owed these guys something."

"It was never a problem here in the old days. It could become one, though."

"The merchants' Mafia," Curly said. He laughed. Then he stopped laughing.

"Sam, I get the impression you're deliberately steering clear of talking about Poirier."

"I've been thinking about your theory."

"But you don't buy it."

"How can I decide? You didn't finish it."

"What do you mean? I told you how I think he killed Prentice. And I showed you how everything added up."

"You didn't explain it all."

"How do you mean?"

"I mean the complete bollix out there after Prentice was killed. Let's give the devil his due, Curly. Pepe is no fool." Sam tapped the side of his head with his forefinger. "Up here he's about as shrewd and tricky as they come. How can you associate the fine hand of Pepe with that bungling mess we found out there? That's not Pepe's work."

"That's the point, Sam. Exactly. You're thinking exactly what Pepe wants you to think."

"Oh?"

"Sure. Like you say—it's a bollix. A mess. Looks just like some jealous boy friend or husband killed Prentice and then went all to hell trying to cover it up. And that's exactly what Pepe wants you to think." He slowed down as they drew near the Civic Building. "And that note from the mysterious *B*. That's part of the act, too. I'll bet you can check every lounge in the valley— every lounge between here and San Francisco—and you're not going to find the woman who wrote that note."

He stopped the car.

Sam sat there in silence for several seconds, then opened the door. "I've got an uneasy feeling you might be right about that note, Curly."

"And about the rest?"

"Well, you sure give Pepe credit for being a pretty quick-thinking cool-headed clever sonofagun."

"I don't underestimate him. Not for a second."

"And we've already got him locked up. Guess you can't ask for much more than that tonight, eh?"

"Guess not." Curly grinned and drove away.

Sam didn't buy Curly's theory.

For one thing: if Pepe was such a quick-thinking clever sonofagun, why had he set up such a beautiful picture for them —and then buggered the whole picture up by stealing the wallet?

For a second thing: there was no way, if Pepe had killed Prentice, or even knew he was dead, no way Pepe would have held onto those credit cards. Hell, to do that a guy would have to be completely bone dead stupid.

Credit cards! He had forgotten them. They were on the front seat of Curly's cruiser. Better give Curly a call and remind him about that.

16

He let himself into the building.

Justine came out of her office. The sight of her startled him. She had taken the ribbon from her hair and it hung carelessly around her shoulders. The three top buttons of her shirt had come undone, revealing the cleft between the swells of her full breasts and a portion of the white brassiere. Her jodhpurs clung damply to the inside of her legs. She looked like an abandoned sex symbol for a riding academy.

But not up close. Up close you could see the moistness of the eyes, the weariness and the grief.

"Gertie has taken a turn for the worse," she said.

"I'll get your car and bring it around to the front."

As he turned she asked, "Where's Curly?"

"Gone home."

"Oh. . . ."

"Why, Justine? Something . . . ?"

"Somebody mentioned you spent all last night in your car. Sam, wouldn't you like to go to bed?"

He grinned. "Well, now," he said, "if that's in the way of being a proposition. . . ."

She picked it up just like in the old days. "A man who hasn't been to bed for thirty or forty hours? What good would you be to a girl?"

"You know the answer to that one," he said.

She seemed about to say something. But she didn't.

She was waiting in front of the building when he brought the car around from the parking lot. He held the door open for her. She hesitated, then slid behind the wheel. She drew the door closed and rolled down the window.

"Sam?"

He leaned down so that his head was at the open window. She tapped the steering wheel nervously. "Oh, never mind."

"You've got something you want to tell me?"

"I guess not. We're both too bushed."

"Well, now, doggone it, that might depend on what you had in mind."

"I didn't have in mind what you would like to think I had in mind. I have something I would like to discuss with you. But it had better wait until—maybe tomorrow."

He didn't pursue it further, and after another moment of hesitation she drove away.

It had been close. She had come very near to confiding in him, telling him what it was that was eating at her. He hadn't pushed it because he knew better. She was too much like her old dad. You try pushing a Marshal and right off he becomes stubborn and defensive and maybe even a little ornery. No . . . what she had to say she would say in her own time.

But he knew it was bothering her plenty. Her mind had been so completely preoccupied that she hadn't even inquired as to what had developed out at the Mink girl's car. And either deliberately or otherwise—he wasn't quite sure himself—he had neglected any mention about the credit cards. Not that it mattered. He would have the credit cards on her desk first thing in the morning. After that . . . just how much control would he have over this situation after that?

The silence within the Civic Building left him with an unexpected sense of loneliness. In retrospect he wondered if maybe he hadn't missed out on a good thing. And by the time he reached his office he had half convinced himself that, handled properly, Justine would have agreeably shared this cot with him for the remainder of the night. He was virtually certain that, had this happened, sometime during the night she would have told him what she had come very close to telling him out there in the car. And he wondered if, with her hair turned loose in that sexy way and the front of her shirt unbuttoned like that, if, either consciously or unconsciously, this wasn't what she had angled for.

But he couldn't be certain. And he hadn't wanted to overstep his mark.

He had taken Justine's hymen when she was sixteen. For the next two years their sexual relationship had been close and frequent. When she was eighteen he had asked her to marry him. She had turned him down. She was too young, she said, and there were too many things she wanted to see and do before she settled down to marriage. First thing she wanted to do was finish school. She'd graduated, age nineteen, and Sandy had financed her to a trip around the world. (That was the year Trixie Belman—then Trixie Sedgewick—and Hector Prentice's daughter Corrine took their European tour, and Sandy wasn't going to have his daughter outdone by "those goddamned high-tones.") When she returned from the tour she immediately entered UCLA. Between the first and second term she had come home and worked as her dad's secretary. But thereafter she spent her summers working in L.A. She graduated with a B.A. and joined the L.A. police department. About the only time he saw her was at Christmas time. But two Christmases ago she had brought somebody home with her. That cut whatever little had remained between them. She had returned to Titan three months before her dad's death. But she had offered Sam no encouragement. He knew she was corresponding with somebody in L.A. Then she had been elected sheriff. The guilt of having stolen the job from him, compounded by a lack of certainty as to her own merits for the job, had caused her to erect a brick wall between them. But he understood and had patiently chipped away at the wall. Today, more than at any time during these past six months, that wall seemed about to crumble. Not that he nursed any great hopes of rekindling the childhood flame she had once carried for him. He was almost convinced she was one of those women who would never shackle herself to any man. But he wanted them to have a good working relationship. And, if possible, something even a little more than that. Her sex drive was strong and demanding. She couldn't go on indefinitely submerging it in work.

He phoned the hospital and identified himself. "I understand

Gertie Hancock has taken a turn for the worse. Is Doc Blainsworth there, by any chance?"

"Doctor Blainsworth is having a cup of—no, here he comes
now. One moment."

Doc was on the line, sucking at something in his teeth and
bellowing an impatient hello. Sam asked how Gertie was. Doc
told him she wasn't good, "damn it!"

Sam got right to the point. "Earlier today you suggested to
me it would be best if we could delay things. Remember?"

"Yeah. You mean about—"

"That's as clear as I want to make it through that switchboard.
Okay?"

"Right. Yeah, I know what you're talking about."

"Now give me a straight answer, Doc. After you talked to me,
did you get in touch with the Sheriff? Did you put that same
suggestion to her?"

"Hell, no. You explained how the situation had to be. Why?
Do you figure she's—?"

"I just wanted to be double damned sure, is all."

"Something not going right down—?"

"And one more question, Doc. A Mrs. Dibbs?"

"Rebecca Dibbs. What about her?"

"She says you've been treating her."

"Sure. Aortic stenosis."

"The heart?"

"Yeah. She caught rheumatic fever when she was a small kid.
Her godsend has been those flowers. Gentle exercise. Like that.
What about her?"

"She claims she saw somebody assault somebody. We can't
find anything to back it up. Is she the kind of person to fabricate
a thing like that? You know. For attention, maybe?"

"I doubt it, Sam. Not Becky. She's queasy about what people think. If she said she saw it she probably thought she did."

"Thought?"

"Imagination, maybe. She watches a lot of those thrillers on TV. Could be her imagination. After all, she's getting on in years."

"Yes," said Sam. "She must be almost as old as you are."

"You're getting to be a smart-assed young sonofabitch."

"Guess I spend too much time with my elders."

"Hah! Go to bed and get some sleep or we'll end up hauling you in here on a stretcher."

"Goodnight, Doc."

Sam dialed Curly's number to remind him about those credit cards, but the line was busy. Probably talking to his wife in Bristow. Hell, she'd only been gone a day. But maybe when you're used to having a woman around you get like that.

He was about to leave the office when the phone rang. It was Rebecca Dibbs.

"I know how it was," she exclaimed. "I've been thinking about it and now I know how it was I saw that man hit that man. When I first heard the choking sound and looked around the hedges I didn't see a thing. Then all at once, just like somebody had turned on a TV, there they were facing me. And I know now why that was. It was because right at that moment a car swung onto the street way back behind them about two blocks and they were outlined in the light from that car. That's how I saw them. And I *did* see them."

He told her he believed her and that first thing tomorrow the sheriff's office would be around there to check up on things real good. He hung up, impressed with the determined sincerity in her voice. Maybe, after all, there was substance to what she said. And that was the hell of this job. You came into contact with so many grifters, were told so many lies, saw so much that was sleazy, that in time you began to put a question mark behind almost everything that was told to you.

17

He left his small cubicle of an office, proceeded along the corridor to the door leading downstairs to the cell-block. As he opened the door he heard a voice.

Schuyler Kleinfeld!

Enraged, he started down the stairs three at a time. He was almost to the bottom before he stopped himself.

Schuyler wasn't down here.

It was the radio.

Sam continued slowly down the steps, listening as he moved.

"—Prentice. Although it is not possible to give details at this time, Conrad Sumner, the district attorney, stated that his department would shortly announce some unexpected developments. Sheriff Justine Marshal was unavailable for comment. However, First Deputy Sam Powell, speaking for the sheriff's office, refused to issue a statement of any kind. To the moment that's the news. Stay tuned for news as it happens."

Sam cursed under his breath. *Unexpected developments!* What was wrong with Sumner's head?

Apparently Sam's footsteps didn't make much sound. Pepe didn't hear him approach. The ex-convict stood clutching the prison bars, staring at the mantel radio on the shelf across the corridor from his cell. His face was twisted in an expression of absolute terror.

When he saw Sam he seemed to panic. He threw himself from the bars and backed up until he was stopped by the wall. He was breathing like a congested pig.

"I'm *innocent!* I didn't do it! I didn't touch him! I didn't see him! I was nowheres near him! Never! Never! So help me God, strike me dead!"

Sam watched him through the bars, not saying a word.

He began babbling, then crying, sinking to his knees. A pitiful sight.

It's never a pleasure to see a man come apart. But Sam maintained his silence.

Pepe walked—crawled—toward him. Sam stepped back. Pepe reached through to him. "Don't do this to me, Sam. Not *this!*" More sobs.

Sam remained silent.

"I was nowhere near the cottage. Ain't no way Sumner can prove I was. Don't let him frame me, Sam. Don't! I got the money from my dad. You ask him. Don't let Sumner frame me, Sam!"

Sam lit his pipe. It gave him a moment to think. "What did Sumner say?"

"He said he could *prove* I done it. You *know* that ain't so. He gets his proof from you. You wouldn't frame me, Sam. I know you wouldn't. I woulda told you about the money you found in the bed, but I stole it from my dad. My own dad, Sam. And I'd sooner go to prison than let dad know I stole from him. But not *murder*, Sam. Not murder."

"You got the money from your dad?"

"Ain't dad seen you? Ain't you talked to him?"

"What did Sumner say?"

"He said he could prove I done it."

"What did he say?"

"He said he could prove I had been out in Prentice's cottage."

"And you deny that."

"I was never near the place."

"Did he say someone had seen you?"

"He never said nothing."

"Did he mention your girl friend, Delores Mink?"

"No."

"Did he say *how* he could prove you had been in Prentice's cottage?"

"No, he . . ." A sudden look of cunning narrowed the ex-convict's eyes. "You talk like you don't know anything about this." He slapped the bar with his open hand. "I *knew* you wouldn't frame me. I *knew* that guy was bluffing."

"He isn't bluffing. So far as the public knows, Prentice's death was an accident. The fact that Sumner admitted to you it wasn't means that he's got you, Pepe. The fact that he issued a statement to the radio implying that the death was anything other than an accident means he's really got you."

"No. I got that money from my dad."

"Your dad can't help you this time."

"You talk to him."

"Pepe," Sam said. "Your girl friend ditched the car. *We found the car.*"

Poirier guarded his expression warily.

"Your girl friend didn't pull it off," Sam said. "When you destroyed Prentice's wallet . . . you should have destroyed *everything!*"

Poirier's face blanched.

"You had better tell me how you got that wallet."

"I'm being framed!"

"Burglary, even robbery—that's one thing. Murder is something else again. You better tell me how you got that wallet."

But the ex-convict refused to speak.

"There's an easy way to clear yourself in my mind," Sam said.

"Yeah?"

"Tell me what you were doing Thursday night about midnight."

"That's the hell of it," Poirier cried. "I was just driving around. By myself. Delores was—uh—working. I was driving around. I ain't *got* no alibi."

Sam's steely eyes probed the convict's. "One chance, Pepe. Where did you get Prentice's wallet?"

"I don't know what you're talking about."

"I'll be back down here at five-thirty this morning. Maybe by then you'll want to talk. But if you've got a story for me, be sure it's the goddamned truth. For your sake, Pepe. Not for Sam Powell's."

He left.

He returned directly to his small cubicle of an office, dialed a number and got an immediate answer.

"Conrad Sumner speaking."

"Sam Powell."

"Oh. A little late to be calling, isn't it?"

"What have you got on Pepe Poirier?"

"What*ever* I have is out of your hands and no longer any of your concern."

"I'm solving a homicide here. You're damned right it's my concern."

"As far as I'm concerned it has already been solved. Good—"

"Listen a minute. If you have Pepe arraigned for Prentice's murder you'll be making the biggest mistake of your political life."

"Is this another of your threats? Before you say anything further I think I should advise you that this call is being recorded."

"I don't care if it's being recorded. I'm not threatening you. I'm trying to get you to understand. This is more involved than you seem to realize. At least let's discuss—"

"You had your chance to discuss. You passed it up."

"Then at least tell me what you've got on Poirier. Maybe I can interpret it—"

"What I've got doesn't need interpretation. Certainly not yours. Goodnight!"

He hung up.

18

Sam was bone weary and mad as hell. Damn Sumner. With the Prentice interests involved he was making every effort to take command and run this show. His overeagerness and determination might cause him to sidestep his usual caution and jump into this thing half-cocked. That could reflect badly, not only upon himself, but also upon the sheriff's office.

He rolled out the office cot and was about to unlace his shoes when he remembered that he hadn't yet contacted Curly. He dialed the number. The line was no longer busy. But he received no answer. He was disturbed. It was no concern of his what Curly did after hours, but he didn't like the idea of his driving around someplace with those credit cards lying unnoticed on the seat beside him.

He was about to go out front and call through on the two-way when he heard the entrance door open. He stood, silent. The footsteps began approaching down the corridor. His door was partially open. He moved quickly to the wall beside the door. He would not be seen by anyone passing down the corridor. As the footsteps approached he mentally clicked off the number of people who had keys to this building: he and Justine and Sumner had keys. Each of the deputies had a key. Oscar Quibell had a key. . . . That was all.

The footsteps stopped outside his door. There was a knock. "Anybody home?" It was Curly.

"Hide under the bed, girls," Sam said in a loud voice.

Curly popped into view, grinning. "You forgot something," he said and gave Sam the four credit cards still wrapped in the handkerchief.

Sam placed the packet on his desk.

Curly gave an appreciative glance at the cot. "That'll feel good," he said, and without another word flopped down on it. "Be seeing you, Sam."

Sam blinked. "Hey, Curly. I'm bushed. I just made that thing down. I had damned little sleep last night."

"Sure. That's . . ." Curly sat up. "You don't know then—about me coming down here?"

"What do you mean?"

"Oh, oh," Curly exclaimed. "That kinda puts a crimp in things. It's a damned good thing I got here when I did, though, or it would have been embarrassing as hell, eh?"

"Say something I can understand."

"Well," Curly explained, "Justine phoned and said because you had sat up all last night in the cruiser I should come down and relieve you so you could go home and be sure of at least a few hours of uninterrupted sleep."

Sam frowned. "She said that?"

"The hell of it is," Curly said, "that kind of puts the *kee-bosh* on your plans, doesn't it? The back seat of the cruiser is sure no place for it."

"What are you talking about?"

Curly grinned. "Don't be so damned shy about these things, Sam. I saw your girl friend sitting out there in your car."

"Now?"

"Yes," Curly mimicked. "Now." He snapped his finger. "Take her up to my place," He spouted. "Sure. No arguments now. You can't take her up to *your* room."

"Curly—"

"None of that now. Is she on the pill?"

"I don't know."

"Well, if she's on the pill there's clean sheets on a shelf in the clothes closet. I'll phone you if anything comes up. If not, what time do you want me to wake you?"

"Uh—five o'clock," Sam replied dazedly.

"Then it's set!"

Justine was sitting in Sam's cruiser smoking a cigarette. She had exchanged the jodhpurs for a very unofficial looking dress. "Sam," she said, "Mom has gone to the hospital to be with Aunt Gertie. I'm in bad need of company."

19

The body was awkward and difficult to handle. But he had managed to maneuver the car down to within a few feet of the boathouse, so that helped. He pushed her partway into the back seat, then went around to the other side and pulled her the rest of the way in so that the upper portion of her body was propped up on the seat. Much the same position she had taken at the time of her death. He studied her in the illumination of the dome light. The under-part of the body—the part you couldn't see now—had turned all blue and ugly. But the face, the breasts, the tummy had taken on a pale, saintly appearance. Death had erased that wanton look and bestowed upon her an appearance of innocent beauty. And even as he considered this thought, the body moved and the legs opened slightly to form a sickeningly enticing familiar V. The acerbic thought came to him that old habits die hard. An anger fomented within. He went to the trunk of the car and retrieved a screwdriver. *Screw . . . driver.* A gratifying twist in semantics seemed to transform this ignoble tool into a weapon of justice. He rammed the tool into that insatiable vulva. No longer was the invitation open to all comers. There rushed a fulminant sensation of victory, of gratification, and his body trembled.

He drove west from Titan, up the WaShaw road, turned onto a side road and traveled for about two miles. He stopped next to a partially cleared field. It was very dark out there, but he was familiar with the terrain. He had selected this field earlier in the day. It would be perfect. Carry the body just beyond the clearing and into those trees. Men worked almost daily in this field. It was likely the body would be discovered within the next two or three days. Perfect. If it was not discovered accidentally, then he would manipulate events so that it would be discovered in time to culminate his overall plan.

Off in the distance a wolf wailed its eerie nocturnal cry. It echoed against the nearby slopes and was picked up at a distance by its mate. There was a time when this sound would have terrorized him. But that was before he had discovered this new indomitable strength which he possessed. Not a physical strength, but a mental strength. That strength which comes to some men in a time of crisis. The strength which ultimately separates the victor from the loser.

He opened the rear door of the car. He took the body in his arms, and as his fingers touched the flesh the thought came to him that he was taking an unknown risk. He must not make mistakes. Only fools made mistakes. Up the road about two miles was a clearing in the trees known as lovers' lane. Supposing someone were parked up there right now. Supposing someone should come from there while he was placing her in the trees and see his car parked on the road . . .

Check!

He drove up the deserted road until he came to the opening into lovers' lane. Slowly he turned the car into the clearing. There were no cars. There was nobody. They were alone.

He turned off the headlights.

20

Sam turned a corner.

"There's nobody following us," she said. "Do you really think Kleinfeld was following us before when we went down to that abandoned car?"

"He suspects something's in the wind."

Sam swung into Curly's driveway and drove into the garage. He got out, went around and opened the door for her. She stepped out and staggered. He placed his arm around her.

"I'm still tight," she said. But he had his doubts about that.

The front door was locked.

He returned to the car and used the two-way radio.

"Car Powell to home." He repeated it. Later he wondered why the hell he hadn't used the telephone, which would have taken him directly into his office.

"Yes, Sam," Curly said.

"Where's the key to your door?"

"Sorry about that. There's a spare under that brick by the step."

Under the brick by the step.

He found the key, unlocked the door, replaced the key under the brick.

They stepped into utter darkness. He groped for the switch. She touched his arm.

"You don't suppose Curly suspects it was *me* in the car?"

"Not a chance."

"Sam . . . ? Those other times . . . I mean, you know, before I went to L.A. You never mentioned— They were just between you and me—right?"

"Between you and me."

He turned on the light, went through to the kitchen and made the drinks. When he returned Justine had substituted the harsh overhead light for the dim glow of a reading lamp.

Sam handed her a drink. "Earlier in the evening," he said, "you wanted to tell me something. What?"

"Sam," she said peevishly, "I didn't come over here to be pumped."

The bedside rug felt soft beneath Sam's feet. Justine came to him in the semidarkness and he lifted her gently into his arms.

The phone rang.

"Just called to see if everything was satisfactory," Curly said nonchalantly.

Sam grinned. "Sorry to have to tell you this, Curly, but your timing was all out."

"Smartass."

Sam hung up the receiver. But Justine reached across, lifted it from the cradle and set it on the table.

"Don't let us forget to put that phone back on the hook," he said.

"Mmmm," she murmured.

21

Shirley Cameron awoke in a panic.

She jumped from the bed and was almost out of the bedroom before she realized what she was doing or what had awakened her. Curly had been killed by an explosion. It had been a vivid, terrifying dream, and though it was the workings of her subconscious mind, it had been more than mere symbolism. The true meaning was right there.

Something had bothered her all evening. Unable to pinpoint it, she had gone to bed with a troubled mind. Now she knew what it was. And she was very frightened.

Unable for the moment to remember where the light switch was situated, she stumbled desperately through the unfamiliar darkness of the hallway, not wishing to waken her sister, yet unwilling to take the time necessary for silence. She kicked over a vase. She struck the wall. She reached the telephone.

Pull yourself together. She found the light switch, dialed the area code, then the number of her own home back in Titan.

The line was busy.

Busy! But how could it be busy at this hour of the morning? It was three o'clock. Getting a better control on herself, she dialed the number again. Slower this time. Very carefully.

The line was busy.

In a complete funk her mind lost its footing and she was incapable of rational thought. She stared at the receiver in her hand, mesmerized by the ominous monotony of the busy signal.

She had visions of Curly lying dead, surrounded by the debris of their home. And it would be her fault.

Their water heater operated on fuel oil. When it was functioning properly, the thermostat cut back the fuel supply when the water reached a point just below boiling. But the thermostat had become faulty, and because the heater was outdated, it was impossible to replace the thermostat assembly. Curly had

wanted to get a new heater immediately. But she had talked
him out of it. The price of the heater would take most of the
money she had been putting away for her new chesterfield
suite.

"I don't like it, Shirley," he had said. "I've seen what can
happen when one of these things overheats and blows up. It's
like a charge of dynamite. And that heater is right under our
bedroom."

"Don't worry," she said. "I'll watch it. I'll light it mornings
and turn it off when the water is hot."

For a couple of weeks Curly had double-checked on the
heater. Eventually he had conceded that she could be trusted
with the responsibility.

It became a matter of habit. Almost. Curly didn't know it, but
one day she had forgotten. She first realized it when, turning
the hot tap, she was met by a belching cloud of steam. She
turned on all the hot taps in the house to release the pressure,
and pretty soon the whole place was like a steam bath. The
sound of the vibrating water pipes frightened her so badly she
ran from the house and hid in the garage. But nothing blew up,
and twenty minutes later when she reentered the house the
steam was gone and cold water ran from the taps.

That was the last time she had ever neglected the heater—
except for yesterday. She had come to Bristow without turning
it off!

Regaining a degree of control, she once more dialed the number.

Busy!

She got another idea. Phone the sheriff's office. That's probably who Curly was talking to anyway. And three calls could be
taken in there at once. If one phone was busy, another would
ring. She knew the number by heart. She dialed it and listened
gratefully to the ringing at the other end.

It rang one hundred times. But nobody answered.

She tried home again. Still busy. She dialed Sam Powell. No answer there either. She thumbed through the district phone book and dialed Justine Marshal.

Aida answered.

"Is Justine there?"

"She's sleeping."

"I'm trying to contact Curly, but there's something wrong with the phone. It's been busy for fifteen minutes. Aida, it's very important. I forgot to turn off the water heater. It could blow up any minute. It's right under the bedroom."

"Good heavens. I'll have Justine drive over right this minute."

"Please have Curly call to let me know he's all right."

"I will, dear."

Aida went upstairs. Justine was not in her room. The bed hadn't been slept in. Her jodhpurs and checked shirt were neatly folded on the chair near the window. Her purse was gone, but the heavy ring of keys and the small .22 caliber pistol which she carried in the purse were sitting on the dresser.

She hurried downstairs, phoned Justine's office. No answer. She scurried back upstairs and got the ring of keys from the dresser.

There was still a light at Wilbur's. She ran across. Wilbur hadn't yet put on his pajamas. He was holding a large knife in his hand. "Been drinkin' coffee and whittlin'."

She requested that he drive her to Curly Cameron's house and suggested they go by way of the Civic Building.

"Just in case," she said.

As they drew near the building she instructed him to slow down. Then, "Stop, Wilbur! That's Curly's cruiser parked there."

Aida was too old to run. But she hurried as best she could. She knew the door would be locked, so she immediately pushed the button for the night bell. She jiggled impatiently at the door.

Nobody. She produced Justine's ring of keys, selected the proper one and unlocked the door.

There was no light in Justine's office, but Sam Powell's door was ajar and light issued from there. She waddled down the hall, pushed the door open, stepped inside and then grabbed the doorway for support. But she was made of good stuff. She stared only a moment at the sickening mess on the floor before proceeding to the phone. She called Doc Blainsworth.

"Arthur, you had better come over here to the Civic Building. I think Curly Cameron is dead."

22

4:10 A.M.

Despite the hour, fifteen or twenty people had gathered outside the building. But they were a silent group, awed by an aura of tragedy.

Inside was the bustle. Billy Badger, on instructions from Conrad Sumner, was taking pictures of everything. Phil Silvers, still in his pajamas, was attempting to find fingerprints. Doc Blainsworth was standing beside Aida handing her a glass of water and ordering her to take a pill. Conrad Sumner moved about, obviously trying to deduce some meaning from this unexpected complication. Schuyler Kleinfeld was also there, keeping to the background, saying nothing, but missing nothing.

Curly Cameron had *not* been killed—no thanks to the miscreant. Someone had smashed him viciously across the side of the head, rupturing the skin and splitting the skull. He had been rushed by ambulance to the emergency ward of the hospital, where younger practitioners than Blainsworth were attempting to maintain that tenuous hold on life.

The sheriff's office had been ravaged. The filing cabinet was a mess. Drawers lay helter-skelter on the floor; others hung precariously from their cubicles. Justine's desk had been upended. Papers and files were everywhere. In the outer office a drawer marked *Prisoners' Clothing* hung open and empty. What had motivated this brutal depredation? Unfortunately, there was no one present who could even testify as to what was missing.

Up to this moment Sumner had made no mention of either Sam Powell or the sheriff. Undoubtedly he had been curious as to their whereabouts, but he welcomed this opportunity to initiate an investigation on his own. His first action had been to dash down to the cellblock. But Poirier was still there, sobbing into his hands, patently unaware of what had transpired upstairs. Back at the scene, he had tried to make some meaning from all this but was hopelessly lost.

To Aida he demanded, "Where the devil is the sheriff?"

"I don't know."

"How about you, Silvers? Surely you know!"

"No."

"I think I know," Kleinfeld said. "Both her and Powell."

"Well, why in heaven's name didn't you say so—long ago?"

"I wasn't asked."

"Well, now you're asked. Where?"

"I'll take you there."

"Never mind taking—"

"I think I had better take you there," Kleinfeld suggested cryptically and started for the door.

Sumner hesitated only a moment before following.

"Where *is* Justine?" Aida asked. But Kleinfeld didn't seem to hear her.

"Aida," Blainsworth said, "Wilbur has gone home. Are you going to wait here for Justine?"

"Yes."

"I'd wait with you, but I'm afraid I'll have to drive over and break the sad news to Curly's wife."

"She's in Bristow, Arthur. She phoned— Oh, my God! I forgot about the water heater!"

She told Blainsworth about Shirley's call and together they hurried from the building.

Curly's house was on the outskirts of town, nestled in a growth of trees two or three blocks from any other building. As they swung into the driveway they noticed a parked car. Kleinfeld and Sumner stood at the foot of the steps staring into their headlights. Blainsworth got out of the car and Aida followed.

"Mrs. Cameron isn't home, boys," Blainsworth said. He rushed up the steps, tried the door. It was locked.

Kleinfeld said, "I think you'll find the key under that brick." He reached down, moved the brick, handed Blainsworth the key.

Blainsworth hastily opened the door, found the light switch, flooded the room in light and started for the kitchen.

He got as far as the open bedroom door.

"Well, I'll be gone to hell." His tone was anything but nice.

The others, following close at his heels, now stood beside him.

In the bedroom, on the bed, covers kicked aside, lay Sam and Justine, asleep, totally embraced, naked.

Sam stirred, slowly turned his head and then froze at the sight of them.

"Curly Cameron is in the hospital," Blainsworth said. "Somebody tried to kill him. In your office."

He drew the door closed.

MONDAY

1

The sun rose in a clear blue sky. A slight warm breeze wafted in from the lake. All indications were for a beautiful day in the valley.

Sheriff Justine Marshal briskly entered the Civic Building, chin out, head erect, exhibiting an hauteur and pride she no doubt did not feel.

Sam followed her into her office and closed the door.

Within the sanctity of the office her Junoesque bearing disintegrated and she fell apart.

"Let's tidy this place up," Sam said. "See if we can figure what's missing."

There was plenty missing. Every scrap of evidence in the Prentice murder was gone. The $650 taken from Poirier's room was gone; so were Pepe's clothes.

There was enough anger in Justine now to displace humiliation. She went to her phone, dialed a number. "You go into the outer office, Sam. Use the extension. I want you to hear this."

When the call was answered at the other end, Sam immediately recognized Aida Marshal's voice.

"Mother," Justine said, "you and Wilbur spent most of last night at the hospital. What time did you return home?"

"About three-fifteen."

"While you were at the hospital, did Wilbur leave?"

"Leave?"

"Go out for cigarettes or anything like that?"

"No. We were in the lobby, then we went into Gertie's room, then we came home."

"How long were you home before Shirley Cameron called?"

"Not very long."

"How long, Mom?"

"Well, as soon as I got home I put on the kettle to boil water for tea. I was still waiting for it to boil."

"Then you went right over to Wilbur's and he was home?"

"Yes."

"Thanks. Any more word on Gertie?"

"No. . . . Justine, is everything going to be all right? I mean —you and Sam?"

"I don't think so, Mom."

Sam hung up and returned to Justine's office.

"Well," she said. "Are you satisfied?"

"Satisfied?"

"That Wilbur didn't do this?"

He frowned. "Justine, I never—"

"You didn't have to. I knew what you were thinking."

But she was wrong. He hadn't for a moment considered Wilbur capable of something so calculatedly cold-blooded as this. And he was surprised that Justine should even nurse such a suspicion.

Justine's phone rang.

"Yes? . . . Yes . . . Sam and Curly. That's right, Conrad. . . . Yes. Herman Munsterburg brought the dog over and . . . No, they didn't mention finding anything. . . . As a matter of fact, he is."

She handed the receiver to Sam, saying, "Sumner."

"What is it, Connie?"

"I want you in my office on the double."

"We're pretty busy here right—"

"You'd better get here while you've still got a leg to stand on."

"You'll have to be more explicit," Sam said, borrowing one of Sumner's favorite expressions.

"Credit cards," Sumner snapped and hung up.

"He wants to see me," Sam said simply and started for the door.

"Sam?"

"Yes."

"We've avoided discussing this, and I won't take your time now, but—well, they're going to ask us to resign. Aren't they?"

"No sense fooling ourselves."

He opened the door.

"Sam? Does Conrad want to see you about Poirier?"

"Yes."

"Did he mention the money?"

"Money?"

"I gave him the money."

"The stuff we found in Pepe's bed?"

"Yes."

"Then it wasn't . . . But why the . . . ?"

"He phoned your car last night when I was waiting in it. You were away with Munsterburg and his dog. I answered the phone. Conrad said he wanted to see the money, that he had reason to believe it came from Larry Prentice's wallet. Naturally, I couldn't refuse. I drove up and got the money for him. That's why I left last night."

"Why didn't you say something?"

"I don't really know," she said. And that was all she said.

Sumner sat smugly behind his desk. Self-confidence was written all over him.

Hector Prentice had positioned himself stiffly in a soft chair to Sam's left. He was a large man, impeccably dressed. His face was strong, his eyes piercing. He looked very much like his brother the senator. He exuded the immediate impression of

strength and self-assurance, those concomitants of a lifetime of
money. He scarcely looked at Sam and offered no form of greeting.

Sumner beckoned the deputy to come forward. "You
checked Larry Prentice's cottage for fingerprints?"

"Yes."

"I'm interested to know what you came up with."

"I don't suppose I came up with anything."

"You don't *suppose* you came up with anything. Don't you
know?"

"Care had been taken to wipe off most of the prints. I got a
few. I had them Xeroxed to Washington. We haven't heard."

Sumner smiled. "You haven't heard." He glanced knowingly
at Prentice. "Apparently Washington sees no reason to give
preferential service to the sheriff's office in Titan."

"It was Sunday evening. I don't suppose they keep much of
a staff there Sunday. These fingerprints aren't so quick to check
out as people believe. Besides . . ."

"Go ahead. Say it."

"Nothing."

"You were going to say something."

"Nothing."

"Then let me say it for you. I've heard you say it many times.
Fingerprints are overrated, seldom available, and have proved
to be of damned little value through the years to the sheriff's
office. Correct?"

"You're trying to tell me something, Connie."

"Mr. Prentice and I are wondering if possibly the reason
fingerprints have been of so little value to your office is because
of the way they have been used—or perhaps have *not* been
used."

"On the phone you mentioned something about credit
cards."

"I'll get to that. Believe me, I'll get to that. First things first,
however—"

"If this is police business I suggest we conduct it in private," Sam said.

"Mr. Prentice is here at my invitation. His son has been killed. He deserves to see what is being done to apprehend the culprit."

"It's not customary procedure—"

"Mr. Prentice is not *exactly* the man in the street."

So the cards were smack on the table. All pretense had been thrown aside. Sumner was Hector Prentice's boy and he didn't give a damn whether Powell knew it or not. Which indicated, as strongly as anything could, that Sumner considered Sam Powell to be washed up.

"Now," Sumner said, "I'm about to charge a man with murder. I wish to find out first, however, if you can substantiate what I have already discovered." He leaned forward in his chair. "In your fingerprinting efforts at the cottage I assume that you checked the back wall of the clothes closet."

"No."

"No!" Sumner's face showed utter disbelief. "With everything indicating that Larry had been attacked practically in his sleep, with the obvious fact being that the culprit had gone into that closet and taken out a suit with which to dress Larry, that the culprit had rampaged through the suits in that closet until he found Larry's wallet—with all these things obvious, you didn't see fit to fingerprint the rear wall of the closet?"

"I think in due course we would have fingerprinted the wall, yes. But—"

"In *due course!*"

"At the time I just figured Larry would have placed his clothes on a chair beside the bed like the rest of us do when we crawl into bed with a woman. However—"

Sumner was on his feet. "That's enough of *that!*"

"What are you implying?" Hector Prentice demanded loudly. "What sort of filthy implication is this?"

"I'm implying that your son liberally seduced some woman immediately before he was killed. I'm—"

"Stop that!" Sumner roared.

"You rotten bum!" Prentice ejaculated. He was livid.

"No effort had been made to wipe the semen from the bedsheet. Nor had it been lain on or in any way disturbed after it had dried. Therefore—"

"Damn it! Stop that!" Sumner thundered. He came around his desk. "Have you no thought for this distraught father?"

"And I'm further implying"—Sam controlled his voice—"that if you two sonsabitches think you're going to hide the truth of this thing behind the conviction of an innocent man, then you're in for the goddamnedest hunk of trouble you ever saw."

Sam, in an effort to control his rage, brought out his pipe. But his eye caught the movement. He looked up just as Prentice, livid with rage, swung an open hand at his face. He deflected the blow with the back of his hand, then grabbed Prentice's wrist in the steel grip of his thick fingers and guided him back to his chair.

"If you can't stand to hear the truth, Hector, then don't bull your way into one of these sessions."

"You're *finished!*" Prentice rasped. "Do you understand? You're *finished* in this town!"

"Try not to let him upset you, Hector," Sumner said. "He knows he's finished. It's his way to release his filthy venom in this manner."

Sam went back to his chair, sensing now, even as he had before walking in here, that Sumner was about to display a winning hand.

"You've made some very damaging insinuations, Powell," Sumner stated. "Do you have any shred of evidence to back them up?"

"You know damned well I don't."

"Are you saying that you sat here and accused Larry Prentice of . . . and you have absolutely no evidence?"

"If it will ease your mind, Connie, I'll confirm what you're hoping. Yes. All the evidence was stolen. The sheet with the semen—everything."

"Stolen? But you said you sent it to the lab in L.A."

"And you knew damned well I didn't."

"Then I take it that all hopes you might have entertained of producing a scandal from this unfortunate affair have been nullified? Wait. Where are you going?"

"I've got work to do. I'm not going to sit in here and hassle with you."

"I think it will be worth your while to listen and hear what I have to say." He glanced at his wrist watch. "We won't be long now.

"Now, getting back to where I was. You did not bother to fingerprint the rear wall of the closet. I, however, did."

"You?"

"Well, not exactly me. The state police."

"The state police! You had no authority to bring them in here."

"Let's say I *took* the authority."

"You broke the seals I had placed on that cottage?"

"Exactly. And fortunate indeed that I did. Mr. Prentice, here, has maintained for years that the sheriff's office in this county is outdated, relaxed and incompetent. During my tenure as the district attorney I had come to realize that his accusations were well founded. When the good people of this county saw fit to elect a young, virtually inexperienced woman as sheriff, then myself, Mr. Prentice and certain other responsible citizens in this community realized that the situation had become intolerable.

"When Larry Prentice was killed I was determined that justice would *not* be handled in its customary cursory, lackadaisical nineteen-twenties fashion. So I called on the state police. After you had fingerprinted that cottage, they, with their skilled methods, went in and also fingerprinted it. On the rear wall of the clothes closet they found a palm print. They sent the print over the wire and quickly had a suspicion of mine confirmed. It was quickly ascertained that Pepe Poirier had made that palm print.

"Further, the state police noted that a small amount of talcum powder had been spilled on the dresser. However, there was a rectangular spot where no talcum was in evidence, indicating that something had been sitting on the dresser at the time the powder was spilled. It's customary for a man to remove his wallet and set it on the dresser when he's shaving and changing from one suit to another."

Sumner paused, stared coldly at the deputy. "Do you understand what I'm getting at, Powell?"

"You're going to tell me that the money I took from the leg of Pepe's bed had traces of that powder on it."

"Precisely. Indicating that that money was taken from the wallet which had been on Larry's dresser.

"Now, let me ask you ..." With a dramatic flourish he cast aside a sheet of paper on his desk and displayed the four credit cards containing the indented name: L. R. Prentice. "Where did you get *these?*"

The cards were sitting loose on the desk. The plastic window-strip was missing.

"Where did *you* get them?" Sam asked.

"They were sitting on your desk when we found Curly Cameron."

"Weren't they enclosed in plastic windows?"

"Indeed they were. And the inside folds of that plastic produced some excellent fingerprints. I haven't as yet received confirmation, but a cursory examination of the characteristics indicate that *some* of those prints were made by Pepe Poirier. Now! Where did you get these cards, Powell?"

"Pepe's girl friend buried them in the ground out by her abandoned car."

"Pepe *Poirier's* girl friend?"

"Yes."

"What made you assume *she* buried them?"

"Munsterburg's dog was following her trail. These were buried along that trail."

"When did you discover this?"

"Shortly before midnight."

"Did you see the sheriff after that?"

"You know goddamned well I did."

"Did you apprise her of the fact you had discovered this vital piece of evidence?"

"No."

Sumner grimaced. "Now let me see if I understand this. You knew Larry Prentice's wallet had been stolen. These credit cards came from Larry's wallet. The sheriff had initiated an all-out search for Larry's killer. But *instead* of notifying the sheriff of this vital discovery, you bilk Curly Cameron into sitting duty for you, you get a bottle of whiskey, and you take the sheriff to bed with you in *Curly Cameron's* own bed! Now what in the name of God kind of a sheriff's office do we have here?"

Sam managed to control himself and hold his silence.

"Surely in the name of heavens you have some explanation for withholding this information."

Sam maintained his silence.

Sumner frowned. He rubbed his forehead thoughtfully. His eyes narrowed like a cat ready for the kill. "As I fit the pieces together, Powell, I deplore the portent of what I see.

"Let me ask you something. Do you look upon Booker Watson as a man who can contain a confidence? I think we can agree that Watson is generally considered to be an old busybody; in short, a gossipmonger. Now, we agreed last night in the sheriff's office that we would act prudently, that we would do all in our power to avoid any indication of scandal in this unfortunate situation. And yet soon after that meeting you made a point of deliberately going to Booker Watson and insinuating that Larry had been with a woman at the time of his death. Do you deny that? . . . You can't deny it, of course, because it's the truth.

"Now, it's no secret that you and Justine—and Sandy Marshal before you—have been hostile toward the Prentice family. As a matter of fact, not ten minutes ago you threatened that if I arrested Pepe Poirier, Hector would be in for a 'hunk of trouble.' In the light of this I'm beginning to suspect that you weren't so negligent with your fingerprinting of that palm print as you claim to be.

"I'm suggesting to your face that you deliberately withheld evidence incriminating Pepe Poirier in an effort to prolong the investigation so that you might venomously inflict allusions of scandal and filth upon Hector Prentice and his family through —God help you—the death of his son."

Sam leaned forward. For just a moment it seemed that he might lunge forward. But he held himself. His body was taut; the muscles along his massive shoulders stood out against his shirt like rods of steel. He didn't say a word.

Sumner withdrew a cigarette. His fingers caressed it. "It is my duty to inform you, Powell, that steps will be taken immediately to call a special meeting of the county commissioners. It is my intention to present these facts as they are. On the basis of these facts it is my objective to have the board pass an amendment whereby Titan County may temporarily fall within the jurisdiction of the state police.

"Further, I am taking legal action to have the authority of the sheriff's office revoked until we can have a hearing on the unnatural actions and, uh—behavior, within that office."

Sumner continued to caress the cigarette. "I am not a vindictive man, Powell. I know Hector is not. And, despite your actions and your overt threats, I am inclined to deal with this in a sensible, prudent manner. I don't relish having to air your dirty laundry before the board. It is no wish of mine to sink our sheriff's office into a mire of filth and disgrace. Furthermore, you can negate any necessity for this by simply resigning. I'm making it as simple and as easy for you as that.

"If both you and the sheriff resign, the board will have no alternative but to bring in the state police. And in due course the authority of the various departments of the law in this county will fall into their proper perspective."

The phone rang.

Sumner scooped it up. "Yes? . . . Put him on." He turned to Hector Prentice. "Sergeant Davidson of the state . . . Yes, Sergeant . . . I thought as much. I was confident from my own cursory examination that they were Poirier's. But it's nice to have the confirmation. . . . A note? Yes, by all means. Read it to me."

As Sumner listened, the smug look on his face began to dissipate. He darted a quick, uneasy glance toward Prentice. "It's, uh, undoubtedly the work of a crank, Sergeant." He uttered a nervous, spastic laugh. ". . . Oh? I see. You have. . . . No! No! That won't be necessary. We'll handle that from this end. Thanks for your, uh, help. I'll send somebody over there for it. Yes. Thank you."

He hung up. He drew a smile across his teeth and nodded in satisfaction. But the eyes told the story. They came up slowly. They no longer carried that arrogant gleam.

"Just as I suspected," he said. "Those fingerprints on the plastic covering of those credit cards are Poirier's."

Sam studied him closely and played a quick hunch. "When do you suggest I submit my resignation?"

"We'll discuss that later!" Sumner snapped. "Just go about your normal duties for the remainder of the day. Just don't, for your own sake, attempt to dig up trouble."

As Sam turned away he noted that Prentice was staring at the district attorney with an expression of bewilderment and anger.

2

Sam's office was four doors down the hall. He wasted no time getting there. He noted the large incrustation of dried blood that lay undisturbed on the floor near his desk. Curly's blood. He grimaced, stepped around the blood, went directly to the shift list he had scotch-taped to the wall. Young Neil Flett who had had the day off yesterday was out on patrol this morning. Sam got him on the mobile phone.

"Neil, I guess you heard about Larry Prentice's accident?"

There was a noticeable pause. "Accident? Sure, Sam. Seymour called me up last night when I got back from my fishing trip."

"Well, as usual the D.A.'s office and our office seem to be working at cross purposes. I was in talking to the D.A. a few minutes ago, and while I was there he got a phone call from Sergeant Davidson of the state patrol in Bristow. He didn't see fit to tell me what the sergeant told him. But it shook him up pretty bad. I've got a strong hunch it's tied in with Prentice's accident."

"I understand what you're saying, Sam. You want me to cut for Bristow and talk to Davidson?"

"You'll have to be pretty cute about it, though. I think from what I could gather Davidson has received a note. I got the idea he read it to Sumner over the phone."

"Then why don't I just go in there and say, 'The sheriff would like a copy of that note you were telling the D.A. about'?"

"Sounds about as good as any. Give it a try. Call when you get it."

He hung up and headed directly for the cellblock.

"Where you been, Sam?" Pepe cried. "You said you'd be back at five-thirty."

"Then you've got something to tell me?"

"Sure. I know you're the only guy in town'll believe me, though. I *found* Prentice's wallet. It was lying on the road. Right up there on Suicide Mountain road."

"You stick to that story and you'll talk yourself right into the death house."

"It's the truth."

"I'm going to be honest with you, Pepe. The D.A.'s got you. And good. The state police found one of your prints in the clothes closet at Prentice's cottage."

"The state police! Those bastards hate me. It's a frameup. They didn't find no print. They *couldn't* have. I wasn't there."

"You're going to make this easy for Sumner if you stay with that story."

"Honest . . ."

"Before you lie any more, let me tell you something. We found a can of Plasto-Blast, plastic bandage, in your hotel room. I imagine if you were to spray that stuff over your fingers and let it dry it would be impossible for you to leave fingerprints. It could leave a guy feeling pretty confident. But supposing you were in somebody's cottage, and supposing you were to lose your balance, or get a little careless, say in a clothes closet, for example, do you know what would happen? You just might put your hand out against the wall. And if you did that, Pepe, you just might leave a *palm* print on that wall. . . . They found your palm print on the wall, Pepe. *Not* your fingerprint."

Poirier gripped the bars, closed his eyes. For several seconds he didn't even breathe. Then the fight went out of him with a forlorn, helpless sigh. He opened his eyes. All cunning was gone. All fight. He had been beaten before. But never like this. Suddenly he was no more than a helpless animal, locked behind bars, pleading with silent eyes for help. And in all the world he knew of only one man who could possibly help him or would care to try.

"I'm sorry, Sam," he said. "I broke it. Our agreement. Jeez, I'm sorry. And I deserve to be hit for it. And hit hard. But not murder, Sam! You know I wouldn't have nothing to do with killing. Nothing to do. You know that. . . . Say it, Sam. Say you know it."

"Tell me all about it, Pepe."

"I will. I'll tell *you*. I won't tell those other sonsabitches, but I'll tell you, Sam." He nodded his head vigorously. But when he spoke again his voice was very soft, meant for Sam's ears only. "Sure. You're right. I was in Prentice's cottage. I heard he was out of town on business. I never liked that stuck-up son of a bitch. I decided to go out to his big-money cottage and see what was what. So I did. I went into the closet and found his wallet in one of the suits hanging there. Cripes! I didn't expect to find a wallet. But there it was. So I . . . I couldn't help myself, Sam. It was there—so I took it. That's what happened. That's *all* that happened."

"When was this?"

"Friday afternoon."

"Was your girl friend with you?"

"No. She don't know nothing about it."

"She knew about the credit cards in the spare tire."

"She didn't know where they came from. I told her if I ever got picked up for anything she should cut them out and get rid of them."

"Her car was full of gas, in top running order. Why did she ditch it?"

"The car would have been too easy to spot, I guess. She couldn't afford to get picked up. She's on the list, Sam. Back in Utah. Hooked up in some kind of bum check thing. You check. She was using the name of Ramona Maitland. I guess she knew she'd never get out of this valley if she tried to get out in the car, so she hitchhiked out."

"And that's your story?"

"It's the truth."

Sam nodded, indicating there was a pretty good chance he believed him.

"Now let's go over that again. The suit was hanging in the closet? The wallet was in the suit?"

"That's the truth."

"Who was with you?"

"Nobody."

"Somebody came in here last night and tore hell out of the sheriff's office. They took your clothes. Why?"

"I ain't got no idea. I've leveled with you, Sam. I don't know a thing about what happened up there last night."

"For what it's worth," Sam said, "I think for once you're telling me the truth."

3

As he walked down the corridor he noticed Justine standing, looking into his office. When she saw him she came forward on the double. She looked completely distraught.

"I'm sorry, Sam," she said. "I'm going to have to leave for a little while. It's Wilbur. We're worried sick about him. His nerves are going on him. Mom just phoned. Something happened over there. Wilbur lost his temper and slapped little Bobby. I just know he didn't mean to hurt him. But Bobby fell over and hit his head and started to bleed. Mom says he isn't badly hurt at all. But Wilbur seems to think he almost killed him. He's going all to pieces. Mom is frightened of what he might do—to *himself.*"

"Sure. You hike on over and give your mom a hand."

"Only until Doc Blainsworth gets there. I imagine he'll give

Wilbur a sedative or something. Then I'll be right back. So many things we have to discuss and—do."

She turned to leave. Then stopped. "Harvey Colton is out front. He said you called his wife last night and told her he would have to come to work today."

He nodded.

"Sam, his vacation starts today."

"They'll have to wait."

She touched her fingertips worriedly to her lips. "I suppose . . . yes . . . we'll need all the help we can get. So many things . . . I'll tell him to come to your office."

Sam stood in the doorway of his office and studied the patch of dried blood near his desk. He went to a desk drawer and withdrew a metal tape measure. He was kneeling down taking measurements near the patch of blood when Deputy Harvey Colton appeared. He was not in uniform; he was wearing faded bluejeans and a denim jacket, indication enough that he had not come down with the intention of working.

"Did you hear about Curly?" Sam asked.

Colton nodded.

Originally Sam had wanted Colton to check the bus depot today, to see if he could learn where Barbara Hancock had gone. But abruptly those plans changed. A suspicion that had been nibbling at him suddenly took full bite. He leaped to his feet, brushed past Colton in the doorway and headed down the corridor. "Let's go," he said.

"Sam," Colton said. "I want to talk—"

"Tell me in the car."

Sam already had the engine going when Colton slid onto the seat beside him. He threw the car into reverse, swung around and shot out of the lot.

"Sam," Colton said, "my wife is pretty upset. We've got a trailer rented, we're all packed . . ."

But Sam wasn't listening. "The way it looks from the blood, Curly must have been standing with his back to the door when he was hit on the head from behind. Then he fell forward so his head almost hit the desk. And that's where he was when they found him. He was in his bare feet and had only his shorts on. The entrance door was locked. . . . What does that mean to you, Harv?"

"I don't know." Colton said. He sounded petulant and deliberately uninterested.

Sam continued, "Curly sure as the devil wouldn't have gone to the entrance door in his shorts to let somebody in. So whoever got in got in with a key. I've got a bad notion where that key came from. A lady reported a commotion over by Oscar Quibell's last night. Oscar has a key to the Civic Building. . . . I hope it isn't what I'm thinking."

Colton made no comment.

"Okay," Sam said. "You've got something to say. Go ahead."

"It's about my vacation. We've got a lodge reserved. My brother-in-law from Spokane and his wife are already there. The sheriff assured me—"

Sam had gently touched the brakes. "You refusing to work?"

"I can't *refuse*. But, darn it—"

"You can refuse."

"I don't like you to put it that way, Sam."

"It's how I'm putting it."

"I don't want to be placed in a position like that. If I refuse, then it goes against my record. It makes me look bad all around."

"Larry Prentice was killed. Curly was slugged over the head and is in damned poor shape in the hospital. I've hinted to you that something serious might have happened to Oscar Quibell. And all you've got on your mind is your vacation." Sam sighed. "We should have had this out long ago. It's my fault. So I'll put it to you now, Harv. Whether you refuse to work today or not, you're finished."

Colton stared at him, incredulous. "*Finished?* You're not serious. You have no auth— What I mean is, you can't just shove a guy out like that. I've been working here for over two years. There isn't a man on the staff who does a better—"

"I know that. We all know that. You're the most thorough and efficient man we've got. But you're a nine-to-fiver. You're one of those guys who likes to work by the clock, lives for holidays and days off. There's no room for a guy like that here. And it's a bad influence on the young guys.

"The place for you is on one of those modern new forces in the city where they've got a union, a pension plan and everything that goes with it. You'll make them a good cop and we'll give you the best references a guy could ask for.

"But I'll put it to you like this. If you refuse to work and help us through this mess we're in right now, then we'll give you your severance pay and you don't need to come back. On the other hand, if you decide to stick around and give us a hand until things get back to normal, then we'll keep you on the payroll until you've had a chance to find another job. One way or the other we'll give you top references. You'll make a good city cop."

Colton's face was as pale white as his cuticles. "Does the sheriff know about this?"

"No. But you can go back and talk to her. Say the word and I'll let you off here and phone a cab to come and pick you up."

"This comes as a . . . hell of a shock."

"Shouldn't, Harv. For quite a while now you've been reluctant to do more than you're paid to do. A thing like that can't go on. You know that. . . . Well? Do I call a cab?"

Colton stared out at the passing houses, sighed a whistling sort of a sigh, shook his head. "No," he said.

Sam glanced at him. "I wish to hell you'd worn something that looked more like a uniform."

They swung onto Belton and Sam slowed down. Driving past Mrs. Dibbs's house, he noticed that, although the sun was up full and bright, the porch light had not been turned off and the blinds were still drawn. He didn't like that at all.

When he drew in front of Oscar's he braked to a stop and told Colton to check the back door. The front door was locked. But it was a fairly common lock, and the first passkey he tried did the trick.

No great pains had been taken to set the scene. Oscar had merely been hauled into the house and left lying on his stomach on the floor of the hallway. His hands and feet had been bound by strips taken from the throw-cover of the chesterfield. The binding had been unnecessary. The gray hair at the back of his head was matted with blood. But very little blood had spilled onto the floor. Oscar hadn't lived long after the blow to the back of the head.

Sam opened the back door for Colton and left him in charge while he trotted down the street to Mrs. Dibbs's.

The front door was locked by an intricate Yale mechanism, and Sam couldn't find a key to fit it. He rang the bell persistently but didn't get an answer. He ran to the back. It was also locked with a Yale. He didn't waste time. He put his boots to the door, and it gave after the third try.

The first thing he heard was the high-pitched squeal a TV set gives when it is turned on before the station has begun transmitting sound. The air was hazy with smoke and sharp with the pungent-acrid odor of burned coffee grounds. In the kitchen he noticed the metal coffee pot on the stove, smoke issuing gently from its spout. Boiled dry and scorching. To his right was the dining room. Beyond that the living room. The smoke had penetrated to that room also and wafted in lazy streamers past the lurid eye of the television.

Becky Dibbs had watched her last TV show. She was lying on her stomach on the floor near a well-worn rocking chair. On the floor near the rocker was a large ugly-looking butcher knife. Beside the knife a hammer. There was no indication that Becky had made any last efforts to reach either of them before her death.

4

Sam entered the Civic Building feeling somewhat relieved. Doc had been able virtually to assure him that Becky had died from natural causes; that is, a heart attack.

Oscar? Well, that was another story. He would have the report of the autopsy in due course.

Sam was bothered by Doc's new attitude. Cold and impersonal. Obviously because of last night. He and Justine getting caught like that. He had expected Doc to be more understanding.

He was pleased to see Lena Halbright at the front desk. She was a plumpish good-natured sort of woman in her mid-twenties. She wasn't permanent staff but she was good in a pinch, and they used her when things got heavy. She was familiar with the two-way, wasn't so hot on the typewriter, but was a terrific speller. Furthermore, she had taken the oath of silence, and as near as they could tell she had never gossiped about the workings of the sheriff's office.

He could tell immediately by the excessive bloat in her breasts that she was pregnant again. Number three. She wasn't a loose woman, but like a lot of girls in town, off the small ranches, she had this chronic misfortune of getting herself knocked up. Titan was bad for that. Too bad she couldn't find a husband.

"Oh, Sam," she said, "Booker Watson has been trying to get you on the phone. I knew you didn't want to be disturbed or to have him know where you were, so I told him you'd call him when you got back. He sounded pretty excited."

Sam nodded. "Has Neil Flett tried to get in touch with me?"

"No, not since I came on."

He frowned. He'd had over two hours. Shouldn't have taken him that long to hike up to Bristow, talk to Sergeant Davidson, and pick up that note or whatever it was.

"I'm anxious to get that call, Lena."

"I'll remember that. What about Booker?"

"Sure. Call him. I'll be in my office."

He seated himself behind his desk. It was pretty clear what had happened last night. Somebody had killed Oscar, taken his key, and let himself in here. Then he had slugged Curly and stolen all the evidence.

The phone rang.

Booker was excited, all right. "I think you should come right over here."

"What is it?"

"It's important, I think. I don't think I should say it out loud."

"What's it about, Booker? I'm pretty busy."

"It's about what you and I were discussing last night."

"I'll be right over."

He found the druggist in his small office at the rear of the store.

"I found this pushed under my door." He handed Sam a sheet of paper.

It was common writing paper. Glued to the face of it were letters which had been cut from the glossy pages of a magazine. The letters had been placed together to form words which produced two cryptic sentences: *Where is the blue cozmettics bag that was in Larry Prentice car? Who owned that bag?*

Holding the paper by its edges, Sam studied it. The spelling was blatantly poor.

"Does it mean anything, Sam?"

"Apparently it's supposed to. But there was no blue bag in Prentice's car."

"Maybe it fell out when the car rolled over."

"The ground was searched. There was no bag."

"I'm wondering why the note was sent to *me.*"

"So am I, Booker." Sam glanced out into the store. "You sell cosmetics bags and things like that. Maybe that's why. Did you sell a blue cosmetics bag to somebody so that it sticks out in your mind? Say, Thursday, for example?"

Booker considered the question diligently but shook his head. "I'll check with the staff. Maybe they'll remember. We sell a lot of luggage in here, though."

"Larry Prentice didn't happen to buy a blue cosmetics bag and have you gift-wrap it for somebody?"

"I'll check."

"*Somebody* is obviously trying to tell us *something,* and they think you hold the key. You go ask the staff."

Booker was back in ten minutes. He hadn't learned a thing.

"It could be a deliberate hoax, Booker, just to get some dirty gossip started."

"Why should they choose me? I'm certainly not going to start any dirty gossip."

"We'll just keep it to ourselves then. You and me. If you come up with something, give me a call. Just you and me, Booker."

He took a new notebook from Booker's shelf, placed the note between the pages, and in that manner transported the note back to the Civic Building.

Justine had not returned to her office.

He opened a storage cupboard in her outer office, withdrew a jug of iodine and a pyrex dish. He poured iodine into the dish until the bottom was covered. He located two sticks—about an inch thick and the length of the dish—and placed them on the bottom of the dish. He took the note Booker had given him and placed it on the two sticks so that it was suspended above the surface of the iodine. He brought a sheet of glass from the storage cupboard and set it over the dish.

He took a 35-millimeter camera from the storage cupboard, checked it for film, set it on the desk beside the cake dish and waited. He knew that he must wait about five minutes. In that period the iodine fumes would react with extraneous greases or impressions on the paper and disclose any fingerprints. In theory that's how it worked. However, he knew from long experience that in practice it seldom worked. Through the years he had found it almost impossible to obtain a traceable set of prints from paper.

However, the iodine fumes did have the habit of coming up with some real surprises. Usually these took the form of impressions. Either impressions of something that had been sitting on the paper, or—in the case of paper from a writing pad—impressions from words that had been written on the sheet directly on top of the sheet in question. This had become more evident since the advent of ballpoint pens and the added pressure used in their manipulation.

So Sam, feeling somewhat like a man who has paid his money and is about to draw a string in a carnival fishbowl, sat back and waited.

Lena called him. "Phil Silvers on the line."

"I'll take it in Justine's office."

"Sam," Silvers said, "I've checked every lounge in town. Prentice seldom drank in any of them except the Henry Pike. None of the waiters remember seeing him on Thursday, and so near as I can find out he was never seen in public drinking with any woman except his wife."

"You sure you tried every lounge?"

"Yes."

"How about that little lodge stuck up there by WaShaw Falls? Have—"

"That's where I'm phoning from. I just finished. And let me tell you it isn't easy to ask these questions without raising a few eyebrows."

Sam said he understood.

"What do I do now?"

"We've missed something, somewhere. Maybe the lounge is out of town. Bristow. That's only a forty-minute drive."

"I'll probably need a picture of Prentice."

"Try Billy Badger's studio. He'll have one."

Sam hung up and returned to the pyrex dish and immediately let out an exclamation. Something very significant was happening here. The iodine fumes were bringing out dark impressions on the paper. Definite words were beginning to take shape: . . . *meet* . . . *lounge* . . . *5 P.M.* . . . *Please* . . . *forget* . . . *B.*

He stared at the words in astonishment. Setting the glass plate aside, he removed the sheet of paper and studied it more carefully. He was nonplussed. If he had expected anything from this sheet of paper, he had expected anything but this.

Even as he stared at the words, they disappeared before his eyes. And he was so preoccupied with his thoughts that he didn't realize it was happening. But it didn't matter. He could make the writing reappear whenever he chose.

The important thing right now was that those words—*meet, lounge, 5 P.M. Please, forget*—and that signature *B*, these were impressions from the note they had found in Larry Prentice's pocket.

They had come from the same writing pad.

The mysterious writer *B* who referred to Larry as *darling* had also sent this anonymous note to Booker Watson.

But why?

There had been no blue bag in Prentice's car, nor at the scene of the accident.

But why had *B* thought there was? And why had she risked involvement to bring this to light? What was the implication of this nonexistent blue cosmetics bag?

If there had been a bag, the killer had obviously removed it. Or . . .

There was one other possibility. One other person had possibly had an opportunity to remove that bag.

He picked up the phone and called Henry Pike.

"Henry, I'm trying to get a picture of what happened yesterday morning when you came upon the scene of the accident. You were behind the Belmans?"

"Yes."

"How far?"

"Not more than a mile. I noticed them ahead of me two or three times as we were coming down the road."

"Then you got to the scene shortly after they did."

"Not more than two or three minutes."

"Where were the Belmans when you got there?"

"Trixie—Mrs. Belman—was looking over the edge. Just as I pulled up behind her, she turned and started to get into her car. Then she saw me and told me Kit had just yelled up that there was an accident down there and she was going to phone the sheriff."

"Had she been down to the accident?"

"No."

"How do you know?"

"She couldn't have got down there and back so fast."

"Was she carrying anything? A small case, say? Maybe a camera case—something like that?"

"No."

"You went down to the wrecked car then?"

"Right."

"Kit Belman—what was he doing?"

"Just standing there, looking at the body."

"What was he carrying?"

"Nothing."

"You're sure he wasn't carrying a small camera case or some kind of a case or bag like that?"

"Positive."

"And the two of you stood there waiting until the sheriff came?"

"Right. What's the problem, Powell?"

"Somebody took some unauthorized pictures down there," Sam lied. "I'm trying to figure who it was."

"It wasn't us. I can guarantee it."

"Thanks, Henry."

Sam hung up, sat back in Justine's chair and scratched his head, perplexed.

Phil Silvers's excited voice crackled through the radio monitor at the outer desk.

5

Phil Silvers drove slowly down the precipitous road from the WaShaw Lodge. The road would take him through town and out to the four-laner. He was looking forward to his short trip to Bristow. That new four-laner gave a guy a chance to get rid of that pent-up feeling that builds up. Last time he had come from Bristow he had clocked the cruiser at better than one-ten.

But right now he was traveling rather slowly.

A short distance ahead a station wagon shot out in front of him, veered wildly to stay on the road, and then, rear end swaying dangerously, began barreling into town. It seemed only partially under control.

Silvers snapped on the flashing red fender light, engaged the siren and gave chase.

The wagon drew immediately to the side of the road and stopped. There were two small children in the back. He vaguely recognized the driver as a Mrs. Guzowski. She looked scared to death.

"There's a dead woman!" she gasped. "Oh, my God! She's in the trees a quarter mile past our place. It's *terrible!*"

It was terrible all right.

Mrs. Guzowski's two kids had discovered the nude body in the fir trees about two hundred yards off the road.

When Sam reached the scene, Schuyler Kleinfeld was already there with a tape machine, recording. Silvers was vainly trying to keep him away, but Kleinfeld was holding up his hand for silence and talking into a microphone.

". . . standing not ten feet from where the body is lying. It's a tragic sight, one that sickens and horrifies. This woman is lying—"

Sam grabbed Kleinfeld by the shoulder, spun him around, ripped the two rolls of tape from the machine and stuck them in the pocket of his tunic.

"Damn it!"

Sam pushed him roughly to the side. "Phil, didn't you tell this honyaker to stay out on the road?"

"Yes, but he—he said if I touched him he'd sue me."

"Well, let him sue *me.*" Sam grabbed Kleinfeld and kicked him in the rear with the side of his boot. The newscaster went sprawling.

"You'll pay dearly for that, Powell."

Sam ignored the threat. "I don't want any mention of this death released until I authorize it. Furthermore, I'm considering charging you with obstructing an officer in his duty and deliberately destroying evidence at the scene of a homicide."

"*Destroying* evidence!"

"You deliberately came in here, against orders, and disturbed this ground, deliberately destroyed important tracks—"

"That's not so!" Kleinfeld cried, no longer certain of himself.

"Furthermore, if you don't want the people of this town to have to get their news from the Bristow radio station, you'd better straighten up and damned quick. Now get out to the road and stay there."

Sam turned to Silvers. "How the devil did he know about this?"

"I honest to gosh don't know, Sam."

Sam moved to within ten feet of the corpse and gritted his teeth against the nauseous twisting of his stomach.

"Recognize her, Phil?" he asked.

Silvers gave him a strange, accosted look and only just managed to turn away before he threw up all over the ground.

Sam hadn't meant the question in that manner. But Silvers's reaction was understandable. Who could recognize *this?*

It was impossible to tell how long the girl had been there. But the wolves had found her first. Her nose had been eaten away and the tender tissues of her face had been devoured down to the skull. An eye was gone. Both hands were missing, and the ulna and radius bones of the forearms had been bared and splintered to the elbow. Certain intestinal organs had been drawn out through a ragged hole in the belly and dragged for several feet. The mutilated thighs had been drawn apart into an obscene V, indicating that the wolves had conducted a tug of war with the legs. Flies and bugs were everywhere, and the faint stench of death was being emitted from the gaseous cavities within the body.

Sam took pictures from all angles.

He had hoped for some indication of tracks leading to the body. But that was out. The ground was a thick blanket of pine needles on which there was absolutely no impression.

However, about two feet from the body he did notice two twigs lying side by side on the ground. They had both been broken at precisely the same spot. A heavy foot could have broken them.

"How close did you come to the body, Phil?" he asked.

"Not closer than ten feet."

Sam took a length of paper towel and placed it over the spot. He staked the towel into place.

Doc Blainsworth arrived. His new attitude toward Sam was chilly and impersonal. He inserted a thermometer in the rectum of the corpse, left it there, and began his silent examination. When he was finished, he withdrew the thermometer, checked it, ordered the body to be taken away, turned and departed without another word.

"Outline the position of the body, Phil," Sam said and moved into step with Blainsworth. "A rough estimate as to how long she's been dead?"

Blainsworth didn't break stride. "Less than two days."

"And more than what?"

"I'll have a fuller report in a couple of hours."

"How did she die?"

"You'll get my report."

"I saw you looking pretty close at her throat."

"You'll get my report."

"Give me a guess."

"No guess."

"Doc, hold on. It's no good for you and me to be on these terms. We've been good friends too long."

Blainsworth kept walking, clearing his throat.

"Doggone it, Doc, Justine is twenty-five years old. We've known each other a long time. It's not—"

"I'm no moral prig," Blainsworth snapped. "I realize a young buck has to have these sexual ablutions. But you used damn poor judgment as to time and place. And nothing irritates me more than to see a good man allow a willful pecker to bugger up a good career."

"You think I'm finished?"

"You don't expect that tribe down there to let an opportunity like this go by? I give you one week and you'll be out on your ass!"

"Don't bet big money on that, Doc."

Blainsworth stopped, turned. "You think you can fight them?"

"I've spent a lifetime working for that chair in the sheriff's office. I'll fight them," he said. "And I'll beat them."

Blainsworth's face lit up. "Damn it, boy. You've got something up your sleeve."

Sam allowed himself to smile.

"Good luck." Blainsworth patted him on the arm and started again for his car. He took three or four steps and stopped. "I *think* the girl was choked to death," he said and continued on his way.

Herman Munsterburg arrived an hour and twenty minutes later with his dog.

"We haven't made it very easy for him, Herman," Sam said. "There have been a lot of people trampling around here."

"We let Fritz worry about that. We start with the girl, eh?"

"Okay."

"No clothes at all, eh?"

"No."

Munsterburg led his dog to where the body had lain. All that remained now, of course, was a grotesque caricature etched in hydrated lime.

Munsterburg directed his dog's nose to the spot and gave him the *such* command several times. The dog struck out in first one direction, then another, each time making his advance a little farther than before.

Munsterburg stated, "That woman didn't walk in here, Sam. She was carried. There is no track."

"Then let's try this." Sam led Herman to the spot that was protected by the paper towel.

"Ah, ha!" the German exclaimed. "The broken twigs. Yes. Could be whoever carried her stepped on that spot. Eh?"

This time they struck pay dirt. Moving slowly, the dog cut out in a straight line from the body and parallel to the road. They had traveled fifty yards when the dog began digging.

"*Nein,* Fritz."

The clothes had not been buried very deeply. A small depression had been made and the clothes had been more or less covered with leaves and moss.

Sam brought them out carefully and laid them on the ground. There were a red jacket, a red skirt, a white blouse, filmy red panties, dark-toned sheer nylon stockings, a half-slip, a pair of high-heeled red sandals and a brassiere.

Sam instructed Silvers to watch the clothes while he had Munsterburg continue on with the dog.

Fritz led them directly to the road where the killer had returned to his car. But all tracks had been brushed from the dirt.

"Let's pick up the track he made carrying the girl into the field," Sam said.

"Fritz has got it."

"Take it slow now. The killer was carrying double weight. This is the track that might give us what we want."

The dog led them back into the ditch.

"Hold it!" Sam exclaimed. "This is what I want."

The earth beneath the grass at the bottom of the ditch was still damp from Thursday night's rain. The grass had been pressed heavily into this damp earth in two places, forming two very distinct footprints.

An hour later Sam had sent Silvers to make the rounds of the hotels and motels with a description of the clothes, and Sam was walking into the Civic Building carrying the clothes and plaster of paris impressions of the two footprints.

Lena Halbrite was speaking on the telephone. She beckoned to Sam. "Hold on, Doctor; here he is now." She handed the receiver to Sam. "It's Doc Blainsworth."

"Here's what I've got for you. The girl died roughly two or three hours after her last meal. Somewhere within the last couple of days. Likely sometime Sunday. But I can't be definite on that. Some things aren't adding up."

"But two or three hours after she ate. You're pretty sure of that?"

"Yeh."

"What did she eat?"

"Peas, potatoes, onions, steak."

"Doesn't sound like her last meal was breakfast."

"No."

"Any idea who she is?"

"None. But I think she's a local girl."

"Why?"

"Her dental work. She's got three of those white temporary fillings. Oil of eucalyptus. Not many dentists resort to that, but we've got a son-of-a-bitch in town who's famous for it."

"What do you mean?"

"Instead of putting a proper filling in right at the start, he puts one of these temporary fillings in, telling the patient that if it doesn't ache he'll put the proper filling in later. Then he puts the proper filling in and that way charges them twice."

"Who is he?"

"It's against my ethics to say. But I'll see him myself. Maybe he can match the teeth against his charts."

"How did she die?"

"She was choked to death all right. But here's something to consider. There is evidence of a barbiturate, which means she was probably drugged at the time she was killed.

"And here's something else. There are a few small white particles imbedded in the skin of the throat. They could have come off the killer's fingers. My guess is that they could be a form of plaster dust or chalk dust."

"You've really been busy."

"I like to get involved," Blainsworth said dryly. "One last thing. It probably isn't important. But it should be of particular interest to a guy like you."

"Yes?"

"Either shortly before, during, or after death she had herself a real good piece of tail."

Sam frowned at the telephone. "*After* death, Doc? For God's sake!"

"That's what I think. She's got a bellyful of unabsorbed semen. When the tissues of the body cool, they don't absorb the spermatozoa. So . . . on top of this, there's a bad wound in there that didn't bleed. So I would say she was stabbed and raped after she was dead. Yes. The love-hate syndrome of the necrophiliac. I'm afraid you've got a psycho on your hands, my boy."

Sam hung up, turned to Lena. "Sheriff in her office?"

"She took her mother to the hospital. Her aunt had a turn for the worse."

He went into Justine's outer office, laid the dead woman's clothes out on the floor. He studied them a moment and was just stepping out of the office to order coffee when Justine entered the building. She looked drawn and completely done in.

"Gertie worse?" he asked.

She nodded. "But Curly has regained consciousness."

"He going to be all right?"

"They're optimistic, they say."

That was a relief.

"I talked to him, Sam. He didn't see who attacked him. He has no idea."

She wiped something from her eyes. "What's this I hear about a corpse being found west of town?"

"A woman. No identification yet. Doc figures she died yesterday. Maybe about two hours after dinner."

"That would make it Sunday afternoon."

"We've got her clothes right here."

"I see. Let's take a look. I suppose you have sent a . . ." The words seemed to die in her throat. She stared wide-eyed at the red suit on the floor. Her face turned pasty and she slumped over into a dead faint.

He managed to grab her before she struck the floor. He eased her onto the floor and placed a pillow under her head.

The phone rang. It was Silvers and he was excited.

"We've hit pay dirt, Sam. And it's dynamite. Henry Pike recognized the description of the clothes. The woman who wore them registered in here Saturday afternoon. Get set for a shock."

Sam said, "Barbara Hancock?"

"It was—*how the hell did you know?*"

6

Sam said, "I'll be right over there. Right now I want you to hike on over to Bristow and check those lounges. And if you see Neil Flett up there, have him give me a call."

The Henry Pike didn't have to take a back seat to a lot of those big Florida hotels. Its huge lobby was broadloomed from wall to wall. There was a working waterfall over near the entrance to the dining room, and in the center of the room was a large palm grove with a bright fluorescent sun for photosynthesis. This place had cost plenty. But the activity in the lobby indicated it was probably paying good interest on the investment.

Henry Pike was waiting in his luxurious office when Sam arrived.

"You say Barbara Hancock signed in here Saturday afternoon?"

"Our register shows she signed in at four-thirty."

"Did you see her sign in?"

"No."

"But you *did* see her?"

"I saw her in the lobby, yes. Later in the day."

"And she was wearing a red suit?"

"Yes."

"You've got a good memory, Henry."

"That suit fit her like a glove. A man wouldn't forget it in a hurry."

"Did you talk to her?"

"No."

"But you saw her in the lobby."

"Yes."

"How well do you know her?"

Pike arched an eyebrow. "I don't think I care for that question, Powell."

"Why?"

"I don't like the implication."

"What implication?"

"I've got an idea that the dead woman you found this afternoon was Barbara Hancock."

"What dead woman?"

"It's no secret you found a dead woman."

"Who told you?"

"It's all over town."

"Why do you think it's Barbara Hancock?"

"It's obvious. You've got a woman's clothes and you're trying to find out who wore them. And I know the dead woman was chewed up beyond recognition."

"How do you know that?"

"I told you. It's all over town."

"How well did you know her?"

Pike sighed. "I knew her to say hello to. I also knew her by reputation, and, knowing that, I would naturally stay clear of her."

"What reputation?"

"You know her reputation."

"I knew her reputation before she was married."

"Marriage hasn't slowed her down much—from what I hear. Her husband isn't very bright, you know."

"You must have been a little suspicious then when you saw her in the lobby."

"I was suspicious until I checked the register and found she was a paying guest. It's a policy of the house not to suspect our paying guests."

"It must have made you curious when you found she was registered here."

"I make a point not to be curious about those things."

"Has she registered here before?"

"I don't know."

"Did she have any visitors while she was here?"

"I don't know. But we can ask Lawrence. He was on the desk Saturday night."

"When did she check out?"

"She didn't."

"How's that?"

Pike stared at a rectangular card in his hand. "She signed in here Saturday afternoon. She paid in advance for one night. From what I gather, her luggage was still in her room Sunday night. I was informed that her bed hadn't been slept in."

"Where's her luggage now?"

"It was placed in the storage room."

"What luggage did she have?"

"I don't know. I merely instructed them to place it in storage."

"Did you try to get in touch with her?"

"Of course not."

"Weren't you curious as to why she hadn't picked up the luggage?"

"We assumed she would pick it up when it suited her to do so. We don't question our guests' motives on these things." Pike leaned across his desk. "Here's her card. You'll notice that she made two phone calls. One at five-thirty, the other at nine."

Sam studied the card a moment. "Mind if I use your phone?" He dialed the first number on the card. The phone rang a dozen times before he got an answer.

A pleasant female voice, slightly out of breath said, "Hello?" Sam identified himself.

"I'm sorry, Mr. Powell. Mr. Watson isn't in."

Sam hesitated, then, "Is this the private phone in Booker's office?"

"Yes."

"Where's Booker?"

"At the dentist."

"When will he be back?"

"He said not to expect him before two."

"What time do you make it now?"

"One-fifteen."

"When he comes back, tell him to whip across here to the Pike Hotel. I'll be waiting here for him."

"Very well."

He broke the connection, turned to Pike. "Was Booker Watson in here Saturday night?"

"I don't know."

Sam dialed the second number. The phone was quickly answered and he recognized the voice immediately.

"Trixie, this is Sam Powell."

"Yes." Stiff, formal, unfriendly as ever.

"Did you or your husband talk to Barbara Hancock on Saturday night?"

"Why do you ask that?" Her question came quickly.

"Police business."

"Has something happened to her?" she demanded. Strangely, there was a note of real concern in her voice.

"Why do you think something has happened to her?"

"She seemed to think that—well, something *might.*"

"Then you did talk to her?"

"Yes. That is, in a sense I did."

"I think I'd better come out there and talk to you," he said. "I'll be there in five minutes."

He hung up.

"Look, Henry, if Booker comes here while I'm gone, have him wait. I won't be long."

The Belman home was situated on a private road near the lake. The road rounded a huge rock, and there on the flat below stood the house. It was a choice location and certainly one of the most pretentious houses in the county. Trixie's father, Arnold Sedgewick, the lumber magnate, had given them this house for a wedding present. Sam suspected that Sedgewick's money also paid for most of its upkeep.

Trixie met him at the door and abruptly demanded, "Are you in the habit of upsetting people like this? The *least* you could have done before hanging up in my ear was to give me some indication of what this is all about."

She stayed in the doorway, thereby making it clear that Sam was not being invited inside.

"Barbara Hancock phoned you Saturday night at nine o'clock?"

"Yes."

"What did she want?"

"Has something happened to her?"

"What did she want?" he asked.

"I asked you a question. Will you have the decency to answer it!"

"She's missing," he said. "What did she want?"

"I don't know exactly."

"Well, what do you know about the call?"

"I think she was in trouble. She said she was in trouble, that I, because of my position, was probably the only one who could help her."

"Your position? What did she mean by that?"

"Are you attempting to be impertinent? I presume she meant my position in the community; perhaps she meant my position as president of the chamber of commerce. I didn't question her."

"Had she called you often in the past?"

"Don't be ridiculous."

"Then you *weren't* friends?"

"That question isn't even worthy of an answer. You know very well I wouldn't associate with a woman like that."

"What did she want you to do?"

"She wanted me to meet her."

"And you refused. Right?"

Trixie hesitated. "As a matter of fact, no. I didn't refuse her."

"You agreed to meet her?"

"I *agreed* to meet her, yes. But I didn't meet her."

Sam scratched his head. "Why don't you just do what I asked you to do in the beginning, Trixie. Just tell me what she wanted, and what happened."

"I resent your tone of voice. I resent your attitude. And I resent your giving this conversation the aspect of a third degree."

He said nothing.

She glared at him. "Very well, then. She phoned and said she was in trouble. She sounded very frightened, said it was a case of—well, of life and death. You know how emotional that kind of woman is. She said that I was probably the only person in the world in a position to help her. She said she was at the Pike Hotel, room two-fourteen. She asked me if I would come there, said she needed to talk it out with me, to get my advice."

"And you went?"

"Yes, I went. However—"

"Just a minute, Trixie. Where was Kit at this time?"

"He was right here standing at my side."

"Did he go with you?"

"No."

"I was told this afternoon that Barbara Hancock doesn't have a very—what would you say?—nice reputation. I get the idea you know about that reputation."

"I keep abreast of things."

"Do you suppose Kit knows?"

"Of course."

"What did he think of your meeting a woman of that reputation in her hotel room at nine or nine-thirty at night?"

She laughed in his face. "I'm afraid my husband's mind doesn't function along the same lines as yours. It was, if you care to know, Kit's idea that I go. You see, I at first refused to go. Then my husband and I talked it over and we realized it was more or less my duty to go. When you obtain a certain stature in the community you are called upon to do things that are not always what you might *choose* to do. My husband, for example, is not the head of the Boy Scout movement in this town merely because he has nothing better to do with his time. He has taken that position because it is his *duty*. And that's exactly the way we felt about that phone call from Barbara Hancock. If that girl was in a mental dilemma, as she obviously was—she was staying in a hotel instead of at her home; she was most certainly upset —then I would have been remiss in my duty as a leader in this community not to be of some assistance to her."

"So you went to see her."

"I went to see her, but I didn't see her. We agreed that I would go directly up to her room. She wasn't there when I got there, so I went in and waited. I waited twenty minutes, then returned home. I didn't see her at all."

"Had she suggested that she might not be there when you got there?"

"She did. She said she had to run across and keep an appointment with somebody and she might be delayed a minute or so."

"She said 'run across' to see somebody?"

"Something like that. I'm not positive her exact words were 'run across.' However, that was the impression I got, that she was perhaps going across the street or something like that."

He thanked her, and it seemed that he was through with his questions when he unexpectedly threw another one at her. "Trixie, where were you Thursday night?"

"What concern is that of yours?"

"Why don't you answer my question?"

"I'll tell you this much. If you keep badgering me like this,
I'm going to get my father's lawyers to look after your questions."

"That's your privilege. If you want to call a lawyer, go ahead.
Tell him you'll be waiting for him down at the sheriff's office."

She seemed incredulous. "Are you serious, for heaven's
sake?"

"It was your idea."

"Oh, for heaven's sake. I'll answer your silly question. Where
was I Thursday night? I was right here at home. All night."

"Can you verify that?"

"Don't you consider my word as sufficient verification? I was
alone."

"Where was Kit?"

"Kit happened to be at a unit convention in Seattle."

He thanked her again and left. Booker Watson was waiting
for him in Henry Pike's office when he arrived.

7

Sam asked Pike if he could be alone with Watson.

When they were alone behind a closed door Sam said, "Barbara Hancock used to work for you, Booker."

The druggist nodded. "Years ago. Yes. Gosh, Sam, I was
shaken to hear that news."

"What news?"

"About her being killed like that."

"Killed?" Sam exclaimed. "Was Barbara killed?"

Watson was confounded. "But . . . I . . . I thought she was . . .
Henry said she was dead, that you'd found her clothes—"

"We found her clothes. And we found a dead body. Do you
know of any trouble she was in, why she should want to disappear? Was she in trouble?"

"She left her husband. I know that. She said her husband and her had had a fight and she was never going back to him."

"When did she tell you this?"

"Why, uh—I'm not sure. Thursday or Friday, or something."

"Saturday, maybe?"

"Yes, it could have been Saturday, I suppose."

"Where was she when she told you this?"

"Why, she, uh, she told me on the phone. She phoned me and told me. That's right. It was Saturday."

"Why did she phone you and tell you that?"

Booker was sweating. "Heavens, Sam, you make this sound like a cross-examination or something."

"I don't want it to sound like that, Booker. We're just two friends discussing an unfortunate situation. I've got to ask these questions because I think you might know something that I don't know. If you want to just come right out and tell me what you know, then go ahead. I'll just sit here and listen."

"I don't know what to tell. I mean what there *is* to tell."

"Why did she phone you?"

"What do you mean?"

"She must have had a reason for phoning and telling you that she had left her husband." He paused, then very deliberately stated, "Now then, she phoned you on *Saturday afternoon at five-thirty and*— What's the matter, Booker?"

Booker was staring at him with eyes full of dread. "You know!" he gasped. "You know *everything!* All about it. You're just trying to corner me into lying to you. I didn't tell you she phoned me at five-thirty. But you knew. You know about me coming over here too, don't you? Well, all right. I admit it. I did come over to her room. But it wasn't the way it looked. It wasn't, Sam. Honest to God. I never put a hand on her. Even when she was working for me in the store I never put a hand on her."

Sam casually brought out his pipe and filled it. It gave him a moment to contemplate, and it gave poor Booker a chance to simmer down.

"Now, Booker, I'm not trying to trick you into saying anything. I just want to know what happened. You tell me when I'm right and when I'm wrong. All right?"

Watson nodded.

"She phoned you to come over. You came over at—what time would you say?"

"Six-fifteen."

"Then what happened?"

"She said she was lonesome. She seemed upset. She asked me if I would have supper with her. And I said I would. So we did. And then—"

"Just a sec, Booker. Where did you go for supper?"

"No place. We ate in her room. She phoned out to the Steak Loft and we had a couple of steaks delivered."

Sam rubbed the side of his nose thoughtfully. "I didn't know the Loft delivered."

"They will if you pay extra. I gave them a dollar extra."

"Who delivered?"

"I don't know. I, uh—I was in the bathroom at the time. I gave Barbara the money to pay for it before it arrived."

"Sounds to me like you deliberately hid in there so you wouldn't be seen."

Watson shifted uncomfortably. "You know how people are. I didn't want anybody getting any wrong ideas."

"So nobody knew you were in her room?"

"No."

"You didn't stop at the desk?"

"No."

Sam reflected a moment, then, "What did you have for the meal?"

"Steak."

"And?"

"Well—let me think. Uh—peas . . . potatoes . . . onions. I had toast. Barbara didn't."

"Tell me, Booker, what time did you finish eating that meal?"

"About seven-thirty, I suppose."

"Then what happened?"

"Then I told her I would buy the perfume back and I gave her fifteen dollars for it and left."

"Perfume? What perfume was that?"

"Her husband—Wilbur—had bought a twenty-five dollar bottle of perfume from my store about two weeks ago for her birthday. She said she was broke and needed the money and wanted to sell it back to me."

"Twenty-five dollars is a lot of money for a man in Wilbur's class to pay for a bottle of perfume."

"He was always buying her expensive presents. It's the way he was, that's all. Guess you could say he didn't know any better."

"Where is this bottle of perfume you bought back?"

"Over in the store. She hadn't used only a drop or two. I've got it on sale for nineteen dollars."

The phone rang.

"This is Gilchrist at the desk, Mr. Powell. A Doctor Blainsworth is on the line."

"Put him on. And arrange with somebody to get Barbara Hancock's luggage out of storage. I want to have a look at it."

Blainsworth: "Sam, I've got a report from that dentist. It was his work all right and he recognized it right off. Get set for something of a shock."

"Shoot."

"The dead woman is Barbara Hancock."

"Thanks, Doc."

"You don't sound very surprised."

"We had identified her clothes."

"Oh, then Justine knows."

"I'm pretty sure she knows," Sam said.

He hung up.

Watson shifted uncomfortably. He was perspiring. "It *was* Barbara," he said, ". . . wasn't it?"

"There was barbiturate in her," Sam said.

"So?"

"We're wondering where she got it."

"Was it secobarbitol?"

"We don't know what it was. Why that kind particularly?"

"I brought her some . . . one . . . a seconal tablet. I could tell on the phone she was keyed up. She mentioned she hadn't slept for two nights, wondered if I could bring her something to help her calm down. So I brought her a seconal, told her to take it before she went to bed."

"Would it knock her out?"

"I can't say it would do *that.* It would help her relax. It affects some people more than others."

"One tablet?"

"Yes."

"Had she taken it before you left?"

"No."

"What time did you leave?"

"About eight-thirty. Maybe nine, I suppose. We talked for a while. She was pretty upset."

The door opened and Henry Pike came in with a large lavender blue traveling bag.

"That's Barbara's all right," Watson declared. "I recognize the big gold-embossed *B* on it. Wilbur bought the set from me —maybe six months ago. He had me put the *B* on both the traveling bag and the cosmetics bag that goes with it."

Pike shook his head. "There was no cosmetics bag. This was all the luggage there . . ." Pike's eyebrows shot up. "Say, you don't suppose this traveling bag matches that blue cosmetics bag the sheriff carried up from Larry Prentice's car, do you?"

Sam stiffened as though he had been slapped in the gut with a fungo bat. *Blue cosmetics bag the sheriff carried from Larry Prentice's car!* He tried desperately to control his expression. But Watson was making no effort to control his. He stared at Sam with absolute puzzlement. "But, Sam, you said there was no blue cosmetics bag in . . ." And then Booker sensed he was saying the wrong thing and closed his mouth.

8

Lena Halbright pointed a finger toward Justine's office.

"She's in there, Sam. She's certainly shaken up."

He headed directly for the door.

"Sam," Lena said, "did that call get through to you from Neil Flett?"

"No. When did he call?"

"Just a few minutes ago. I told him you were down at the Pike Hotel and to call there. He must have just missed you. He sounded excited, Sam. Very excited."

"When he calls, have the—"

The phone in front of her began ringing. She answered it immediately, handed the receiver to Sam, said, "It's him."

"Had hell's own time locating Sergeant Davidson," Flett said. "But, boy, when I did. . . . Get ready for a hell of a shock, Sam."

"I've had my quota for the day."

"Listen to this. This morning the state police got a note in the mail saying—here, I'll read it. I've got a copy of it. Here it is:

Why did Barbara Hancock get off the bus in Bristow Thursday? Why did Larry Prentice pick her up? Where did they go?

That's it, Sam. And it wasn't signed. But the state police checked up on it and there's a drive-in attendant across from the bus depot who used to live in Titan. He recognized Barbara Hancock. He saw her get into a blue Lincoln. He doesn't know *who* was driving the Lincoln, Sam. But Prentice's car was a Lincoln. And blue."

Flett stopped for breath. "No bloody wonder Sumner was thrown for a loop."

"No bloody wonder," Sam said and hung up.

He went to Justine's office. She was behind her desk, sobbing into her hands.

Sam closed the door and stood with his back to it. "Justine."

She looked up at him, cheeks red from weeping. "Aunt Gertie passed away, Sam. She . . . she . . . Poor Bobby. Poor, dear little fellow. He has nothing now. *Nobody.*" That got the best of her and she was wracked with sobs again.

It tore at him to see her like this. But his compassion was held in balance by his anger. "Justine, I'm sorry about Gertie. And I feel sorry for little Bobby, but—"

"Sam," she cut in as though she hadn't even been aware that he was speaking, "*was* that Barbara's body you found?"

"Yes."

"And Dr. Blainsworth told you she had been killed Sunday afternoon?"

"At the time he did. Yes. But—"

She squeezed her fists to her eyes. "Please let me be alone for a while till I can collect my thoughts. Then—"

"Justine, there's no time for that. We could be in for the trouble of our lives. And there's no time to collect thoughts. I want some straight, direct answers."

"Answers?"

"Did you find a blue cosmetics bag in Larry Prentice's car?"

She sighed in resignation. "I'm sorry you found out *this* way. I intended—"

"Did you know whose bag it was?"

"Yes. It was Barbara's. She had it with her when I took her to the bus."

"Then you knew she had been with Prentice?"

"Yes."

"And you deliberately concealed this evidence."

"Only because—"

"What did you do with that bag?"

"I put it in the trunk of my car."

"Where is it now?"

"In the trunk."

"Justine!" He was flabbergasted. "Have you any idea what you've done here? You've deliberately concealed evidence in a murder investigation. You believed Wilbur was guilty and you've deliberately concealed this fact."

"Oh, now, Sam. Please—"

"You actually allowed Sumner to charge Pepe Poirier with that murder. You were willing to sit back and . . . and . . . " He allowed the accusation to fall off. He shook his head in utter disbelief. "How far were you planning to let this thing go?"

"I was only stalling for time, Sam."

"Christ, Justine—"

"Gertie was in the hospital. She was all little Bobby had. If we had arrested Wilbur—if something had happened to Wilbur—it would have killed her. I was only hoping to stall things until she got back on her feet. Doctor Blainsworth said even two or three days could make a lot of difference in her chances. I was only hoping for a little time. Then . . . then all of a sudden things got out of hand. It's all happened so fast. I . . . I wanted to tell you, Sam. I . . . things . . . things . . ."

"Justine, Sumner knows Barbara was with Prentice the night he was killed. If—when he gets wind of the fact that you took that cosmetics bag and made no mention of it— Justine, we've got to act fast and—"

The phone rang.

Justine just stared at it helplessly, as though her mind could no longer cope.

Sam scooped up the receiver. "Sheriff's office."

"Sam, is the girl there?" It was Blainsworth.

"She's pretty shaken up right now, Doc."

"Well, I thought I had better phone. I don't know what this is all about, but it don't look goddamned good."

Sam waited.

Blainsworth said, "I'm phoning from Wilbur Hancock's house. Wilbur is dead, Sam. Suicide; hung himself in the basement. . . . Are you still there?"

"I'm listening."

"Then I'll keep talking. Sumner, from what I could get, broke in the door of the house when he found that Wilbur's car was still in the garage. He found the body and called me. I wondered why nobody was here from the sheriff's office. He said the sheriff's office had exempted itself from this case. I asked him what he meant, and he showed me a note he had taken from the breast pocket of Wilbur's shirt. It had been sticking out, and across the top of it was written 'Justine.'

"I can't quote the note word for word, but I can give you a damned good paraphrase. 'Dear Justine, thanks for protecting me and keeping me from being arrested over this terrible thing. I know we've got to think of Bobby first, just like you said, but with Barbara gone, and now mother gone, I just can't stand it anymore!' Then he said that he knew she would take good care of Bobby. And that's about it."

"What else did *Sumner* say?"

"He said that you and Justine were washed up, that he was going to see that this was carried to the highest courts, that you deliberately concealed and aided a murderer."

"Where is Sumner now?"

"I don't know. But he was hell bent for someplace. I'd brace the door if I was you." Then, "Is there any truth to this, Sam?"

"We're in trouble, Doc. That's all I can tell you now."

He hung up.

"Justine," he said coldly, "Wilbur killed himself."

Strangely, she showed no reaction. She had taken so many shocks in the last few hours that she seemed suddenly to have become inured to it all. Her eyes had dried, and the strength of resolution was beginning to show itself on her face.

"He left a note," Sam said. "He made it sound in that note like you had talked to him about the murder, that he knew you knew he had done the killing and that he knew that you were protecting him. Justine—is there any truth in that?"

"Yes."

"You actually *discussed* it with him and told him that you would protect him?"

Rather than answer, she brought a tape machine from the bottom drawer in her desk. She withdrew a tape from her purse and affixed it to the machine. The machine began rolling.

As they watched the tape slowly begin to wind, Justine said, "I went to Wilbur's house shortly after I left you at Larry Prentice's cottage. I took this tape machine. Wilbur had been released from the hospital and was lying down on his bed whittling on a piece of wood with an ugly knife. I remember he held it near his throat when I walked in the room. I was frightened he might use it on himself. I was carrying the small portable tape machine over my shoulder. He didn't realize I was recording the conversation. I just—"

She was interrupted by the sound of her own voice erupting from the tape machine:

JUSTINE: Cigar, Wilbur?

(Pause.)

WILBUR: Thanks, Justine.

JUSTINE: How are you feeling, Wilbur?

(Pause. No answer.)

JUSTINE: They tell me Aunt Gertie is resting nicely. She has shown a lot of improvement since yesterday.

WILBUR: They say she's got a real good chance.

JUSTINE: When is Barbara coming back?

WILBUR: She ain't. She's gone.

JUSTINE: Does she know about your mother?

WILBUR: Wouldn't matter. She wasn't much for mother.

JUSTINE: I mean for Bobby's sake.

(Pause.)

WILBUR: She doesn't like little Bobby.

JUSTINE: He's a fine little boy. . . . He's the one we've got to consider.

WILBUR: Yes.

(Pause.)

JUSTINE: We found Larry Prentice this morning. . . .

(A startled expression in the background.)

JUSTINE: Do you want to tell me about it, Wilbur?

WILBUR: 'Bout what?

JUSTINE: Prentice was choked to death. When he was dying he scratched his attacker pretty badly—we found a lot of the guilty person's skin under his fingernails. (Pause.) That's how you got those scratches on your cheek, Wilbur. (Pause.) The laboratory will prove that, Wilbur. But do you know how I know? I found Barbara's cosmetic bag in the back seat of Larry Prentice's car.

(Pause.)

JUSTINE: Wilbur! Put that knife down. You've got to be strong about this. Think for a minute. Your mother is the one we've got to consider right now. She can't have another shock. She would never recover from it. She has got to live—for Bobby's sake.

(Pause.)

JUSTINE: You haven't admitted you killed Larry Prentice. At the moment I have no definite proof. If you *didn't* kill him, Wilbur, tell me, because I'll have to do what I can to find out who did and remove any suspicion that might fall on you. However, if you *are* guilty, we'll have to do everything possible to conceal this fact until after Gertie is over the hump. But don't lie to me. You see, if you tell me you aren't guilty, first thing I'll do is take a scraping of your skin. If it matches the skin from under Larry Prentice's nails, there won't be a thing I can do for you. Now, I'm willing to go along with you on this, because I'm taking for granted it's little Bobby's welfare and Gertie's you have in mind. If you're guilty, Wilbur, it eventually comes down to the fact that if anything happens to your mother, your son will have nobody. (Pause.) What is it going to be, Wilbur?

(Pause.)

WILBUR: I don't want nothing for myself no more, Justine. Just so's the best is done for Bobby. I'll go along with whatever you say is best.

JUSTINE: Did you kill Larry Prentice?

(Pause.)

JUSTINE: Speak your answer out loud, Wilbur.

WILBUR: Yes. I killed'm.

JUSTINE: Tell me about it.

WILBUR: Barbara run out, said she wasn't coming back, said I could keep Bobby. For some reason I . . . I told her to go ahead. But then I changed my mind. I didn't want her to leave. I jumped in the car and headed for Bristow. Hoped to get there 'fore the bus and get on the bus and ask her to come back. But I was a little late. The bus was just pulling out when I got there. But there was Barbara. I thought she'd had a change of heart herself and was coming back. I didn't want her to see me, to know I'd come after her. Then I saw her get in Larry Prentice's car. I headed back here to home, waited to be here when she got here. But she didn't. By eleven o'clock I knew she wasn't coming back. I drove out near Prentice's cabin and then walked up. I saw them through the window. They were in the bed-room. They were . . . they were . . . in bed. They were . . . you know. I . . . I don't know what happened. I ran in there, pulled him off the wife and—throttled him. I . . . just stood there holding him, till he didn't fight back no more. Then I let go and he fell on the floor.

(Pause.)

Barbara asked me if I was going to kill her, too. I said I wasn't. She said I might as well, that she would be the same as dead when all this came out. So we decided to make it look like an accident. Prentice's clothes were on the chair by the bed, and so, quick as I could, I dressed him and hauled him out to his car. I told Barbara to drive it, then I carried her suitcase down to my car and she followed in Prentice's. We drove along Suicide Road for a long ways, then I set him behind the wheel of his car and let it go over the edge. I drove Barbara to Bristow and left her at the hotel. She said she would leave on the bus next morning. She wasn't coming back. (Pause.) I didn't want her to come back no more, neither.

JUSTINE: Does Gertie know about this?

WILBUR: Nobody knows. 'Cept you.

JUSTINE: Somehow, until Gertie gets over the hump, that's how we've got to keep it. Now I'll type a confession and you sign it.

WILBUR: All right. But ain't you scared of what Sam Powell will do?

Justine reached to turn off the machine, but Sam held his hand over the switch.

JUSTINE: Don't worry about Sam Powell. I'll look after Sam Powell.

He turned off the machine.

"Can't you understand my position, Sam? I had solved the case. I had Wilbur's confession. I couldn't see that anyone would be seriously harmed by drawing the investigation out a few days . . . for Gertie's sake." She looked at him intently. "I only did what I know Dad would have done."

"Did Wilbur sign a confession?"

"Yes."

"Do you have it?"

"Yes."

"Let's see it."

While she was rummaging through her filing cabinet, he rewound a portion of the tape and once again listened thoughtfully. He was in such deep concentration that she had to speak his name twice before he realized she was handing him the confession.

He read it slowly, then handed it back to her. "Burn it."

"What?"

"Burn it."

"No."

"Justine, you have to. You've got that confession dated. Not only that, but you've got the time on it. Eleven-thirty yesterday morning. Don't you realize what's happened since that confession was signed? Don't you realize where this places you?"

"I do." She stood stiffly, her chin thrust forward stubbornly. She spoke as if she were reading a memorized script. "I'm giving this confession to Conrad Sumner. It was always my intention to do so. I did what I thought was right . . . at the time. I had no way of knowing what the repercussions would be.

"I am also submitting my resignation. I see now that it was a mistake for me to take this office. It was never my intention to break the law, only to show compassion within the law."

"The law has no compassion, Justine."

She lowered her eyes bleakly.

"To resign is one thing," he said. "But to give that confession of Wilbur's to Sumner, that's something else again. He'll crucify you."

"I'm not a fool. I knew there could be repercussions. I could never live with myself if I tried to avoid the consequences. I'm not a coward, Sam."

"But I don't think you realize how far he'll—"

There was the heavy thumping sound of rapidly approaching footsteps. Sam ran to the office door and snapped the lock.

There was a loud knocking at the door; the knob turned.

"Who's there?" Sam demanded.

"Conrad Sumner."

Sam walked over to Justine. He took the confession and replaced it in the envelope from which it had come.

"Justine," he whispered quickly. "Don't tell Sumner about this confession until I give you the word. Don't even open your mouth. Let me do the talking."

"But—"

"Believe me, there are more things involved in this than you realize. Promise me?"

"All right."

"Okay," Sam said, "go and open the door for him before he smashes it down."

9

Sam seated himself at Justine's desk.

She opened the door and Sumner came charging in. He was carrying Barbara Hancock's blue cosmetics case. He held it before them.

"This finishes you!" he cried. "Both of you. You deliberately attempted to protect a murderer. And because of that, more murder was committed! I'm going to prosecute you to the hilt."

When neither Sam nor Justine spoke, he looked them over coldly, his passion slowly being replaced by an expression of naked hatred.

"Ohhh, don't worry," he growled. "I've got you. You try and pull one over on me, will you? This is Barbara Hancock's bag. I have a witness who will swear you took this cosmetics bag from

Larry Prentice's car at the time you first went to the wreck. You were seen secreting it in the trunk of your car. And there you have kept it hidden ever since. Until only seconds ago when I took it upon myself to retrieve it. I have a list of your evidence, and this bag is *not* on your list. Further, I have a witness in Bristow who saw Barbara Hancock in Larry Prentice's car the night he was killed.

"You knew this was Barbara Hancock's bag, because I know for a fact that she was carrying it when you, Justine, took her to the bus the day she left town—the same day Prentice was killed, three days before you found this bag in Prentice's car. You knew Barbara Hancock had been with Prentice; you knew Wilbur Hancock had scratches on his face; you knew Wilbur had even tried to kill himself. Yet you deliberately concealed these facts. You deliberately concealed the presence of this cosmetics bag because it would point directly to Barbara Hancock and, consequently, to Wilbur Hancock.

"Not only that, but I state right here and now that you also found a note in Larry Prentice's pocket, that when you realized the significance of that note, that you took means to destroy it." Sumner paused long enough to smile victoriously. "But that didn't work. You forgot something. Billy Baxter photographed that note. I was at Baxter's studio and I now have a copy of that note." He held up a glossy photo. "When the handwriting on this note is analyzed, it will be proved that Barbara Hancock wrote that note.

"You were in possession of all these facts as early as Sunday morning. Because Wilbur was the sheriff's cousin and you chose to conceal this evidence, Wilbur was allowed to run free. And because he was allowed to run free, he was able to locate his wife. He located her, and he *killed* her. And you two are directly responsible for this!

"You're finished! You're washed up! I'm going to prosecute you two to the best of my ability." He swung around and made for the door.

"Connie," Sam said with extreme casualness, "before you go buggering yourself up any further, I think maybe there are a couple of things you should know."

Sumner almost didn't stop. But he had dealt with Sam Powell for too many years to completely ignore him. And Sam's complete self-assurance obviously didn't fit the occasion.

"What do you mean?"

"For your own protection I think you'd better come in and close the door."

"*My* protection?"

"Connie, you brought the state police into this. Because you did, and because of what they uncovered, you figure there's going to be a hell of a scandal involving the Prentice name. You can't make deals with the state police. It's pretty clear to me that you and Prentice have had it out and Prentice has thrown you out, washed his hands of you, because you have precipitated a scandal that's gotten out of control, that's going to make the Prentice name a political football to be kicked across the pages of every opposition newspaper in the country. Now you're going to break your own neck to be certain Justine and I go down with you and the rest of the scandal.

"But you're wrong, Connie. So wrong, you don't even have an *inkling* of what's going on. I've told you for years to mind your own business, to leave the investigation of things to the sheriff's office. Now I'm asking—telling—you again."

"*Bull* shit!" Sumner ejaculated and charged out the door.

Sam waited until he was almost to the corridor, then called, "Barbara Hancock was killed Saturday night!"

Sam allowed himself to look up at Justine. She stared down at him with a look of bewilderment.

Slowly, almost contritely, Sumner reappeared in the doorway. He stepped into the office, slowly closed the door. "What did you say?"

"Check it for yourself. Doc *thought* she might have died Sunday afternoon. But he *knew* that she died two or three hours after she had a meal of peas, potatoes, onions and steak. She had that meal with Booker Watson at seven-thirty Saturday night.

"Now, *you* know that Saturday night Wilbur Hancock was in the hospital recuperating from attempted suicide. So Wilbur couldn't possibly have killed his wife.

"Furthermore," Sam said, "where the hell did you get the idea that Barbara Hancock wrote the note we found in Prentice's pocket? Did you compare it?"

"No," Sumner replied uncertainly.

"Then why did you make such a statement?"

"It seemed obvious."

"Never accept the obvious. I suppose Booker also told you about receiving a note stating that there was a blue cosmetics bag in Prentice's car?"

"Yes."

"Didn't you ever wonder who could have sent that note?"

"What?"

"Who slipped it under his door? The note was supposedly slipped under his door Monday morning—this morning. But Barbara Hancock was dead. So who could have known about this cosmetics case? Who, Connie?"

"Why, I . . . I . . ."

"Could it have been the person who had placed it there in Prentice's car?"

"Placed it? You mean it was deliberately placed there?"

"What do you think?"

Sam got up and walked over to the filing cabinet. He searched out a file until he found what he wanted. He glanced at the first line of the letter:

As President of the Chamber of Commerce . . .

He walked over to Sumner. "You're a pretty good friend of the Belmans, right?"

"Yes."

"When you're together with them, how do you refer to Trixie?"

"By her given name, of course."

"She doesn't like to be called Trixie."

"No. Why these questions?"

"What is Trixie short for?"

"Beatrix, of course."

"And Beatrix starts with a B. Right?"

"Of course, but— Surely to God you're not suggesting that Beatrix wrote this note to Larry Prentice?"

"I'll let you decide that. Here's a letter she wrote this office some weeks ago complaining that—well, never mind what she was complaining about. You just compare this writing with what you have in the photograph of the note we found in Prentice's pocket."

Sumner compared the two samples of writing. His eyes darted from one sample to the other, then widened in disbelief. They were the same hand. "Oh, no," he muttered. "Are you saying there was a love affair between Prentice and Beatrix?"

"I merely give you the facts. You put them together.

"Now answer this question. Who was the first person at the scene of the crime? Who *could* have placed that cosmetics bag in Prentice's car?"

"Kit Belman? Are you saying Kit Belman?"

"I'm not saying anything. I'm just telling you a few of the facts. Now I'm *telling* you to leave this alone and let us keep working on it. You go to Hector Prentice and tell him that things aren't exactly as they seem to be. Tell him that the sheriff's office has come up with some vital new clues that change the whole complexion of this thing, that things might possibly turn out a lot better than he thinks."

"But—"

"You just go and tell him that. And tell him to pull in his horns and calm down. And you calm down, too. And both of you leave us alone so we can keep working on this thing. . . . Leave the cosmetics bag and the picture of that note right here on the desk, Connie."

Sumner did as he was told, then walked dejectedly from the office.

Justine turned to Sam, wide-eyed. "But I don't understand."

"You just keep quiet about this whole mess," he said. "Let me handle it."

"But was Trixie Belman having an affair with Larry Prentice?"

"Of course not."

"But she wrote that note."

"Yes."

"I don't understand."

"You will."

"And Kit Belman—he didn't put that cosmetics bag in Larry's car?"

"No."

"But you told Conrad—"

"I'm letting Sumner draw his own conclusions."

"But you're deliberately tricking him into believing—"

"Your damned right I'm tricking him," Sam said. "And I've only started."

Sam stood up.

"Give me twenty minutes, then phone Trixie Belman. Tell her to come in here on the double. Kit, too. Tell them it's important and imperative that they come. Tell them—now get this—tell them it's about a pair of shoes. Tell them to bring in every pair of shoes Kit owns. Tell them if they don't come with those shoes voluntarily that we'll bring out a search warrant."

He moved around the desk. "Where are those clothes of Barbara Hancock's?"

"In the drawer with the key in it."

He opened the drawer, took the red jacket and deliberately ripped off a button. He dropped it into his pocket.

Justine didn't ask any further questions.

Sam hunkered down in the bushes near the lake. From this vantage point he could see both the front and side doors of the Belmans' house.

The side door flew open and Kit Belman came scurrying out carrying something. He headed straight for the lake. He was coming directly toward Sam. When he was within twenty feet Sam stood up. Belman stopped dead, panicked and began running.

Sam ran after him, gained on him and tackled him. Belman went down hard. He attempted to kick Sam in the face. Sam grabbed the foot, twisted it vengefully. Belman screamed. Sam stood up, placed his foot on Belman's chest.

"You stay put," he said, "or I'll kick your face in."

He picked up the package that had fallen from Belman's hands. It was a sealed pail with holes in it. Sam pried off the top. There was a pair of shoes inside.

"This would have filled up with water pretty fast and stayed at the bottom, where you could have retrieved it later for more permanent burial someplace, eh, Kit? I think these shoes will prove everything we need to prove. But first let's take a look at your car."

"What are you talking about?"

"You know what I'm talking about. But I'll be clear. We found two footprints in the ditch where we located Barbara's body. Those prints were made by the person who carried her body over into the trees. I think these shoes will fit those prints. But let's go over to your car and check it."

"I don't know what you're talking about."

"We're trying to locate a red button. It was missing from

Barbara's jacket. It was nowhere near the scene. We think it might have come off in your car when you—"

"*My* car!"

Sam placed his hand in his pocket and continued walking. "Yes. Your car."

Belman was incredulous. "What possible connection could I have with Barbara Hancock?"

"Never mind the act, Belman. We know everything."

"Why would *I* kill Barbara Hancock?"

"You killed her to protect your silly reputation. She came back to town Saturday night and phoned your wife to come up to her hotel room. You talked your wife into going. When your wife went into town to meet Barbara, Barbara came out here to see you. She told you her cosmetics kit was still in Prentice's wrecked car. Up until then you didn't know where Prentice's car was. Furthermore, I imagine Barbara threatened to expose you if you didn't lend her some money. She was broke. You killed her on the spot. Later you hauled the body out to where we found it."

Belman had the familiar trapped expression of a condemned man who knows fear and very little hope.

They had reached Belman's Mercury sedan parked in the garage beside Trixie's Cadillac. Sam went around to the driver's side, opened the rear door and began searching. In a minute he straightened up, holding a red object in his hand.

Belman stared at the red button and began backing away. Sam walked over to him and slapped his face. "Just wait till I get you down in that cell. You killed Oscar, you son of a bitch. You goddamned near killed Curly. Just wait till we get you down there." He took hold of Belman in his two big hands and shook him as a dog would shake a weasel.

"This is going to be the damnedest scandal that ever hit this town," he said menacingly. "You'll spend the rest of your life in prison."

He dragged Belman over to the car, pointed to a stain on the back seat. "See that semen stain there, Kit? Did you know that semen can be typed with an A and B factor the same as blood? We're going to show that the semen we found in Barbara is the same semen as is on the seat of your car there. And we can damn soon match it with yours.

"When did you seduce her?" he asked dangerously. "Before or after you killed her?"

Belman was terrified.

Sam glared at him. "It's just too bad," he said pointedly, "that you couldn't have a heart attack right now and drop dead and save your wife and the whole valley the scandal that's going to come out of this. It's too bad a mess like this has to go into court."

He turned his back on Belman. "I'm giving you one break, Belman. It's the last break you'll ever get in this world. I hope you've got guts enough to take advantage of it." He started walking away. He didn't look back. "If you're not down at headquarters in thirty minutes we'll be out after you."

He continued walking, went to his cruiser concealed in the trees and drove away.

10

Hector Prentice was in his study gulping brandy. It wasn't his first.

Conrad Sumner was ushered in.

"I couldn't talk on the telephone," Prentice said. "I just heard about young Kit Belman. How did it happen?"

"He was traveling along Suicide Mountain. He hit one of those curves at considerable speed and . . . kept on going, apparently."

"That's too much coincidence to be an accident."

"Obvious suicide," Sumner said. "A clear admission of guilt."

Prentice groaned, cursed. "So what does it mean?"

"Powell claims he will have no trouble proving that Kit killed Barbara Hancock."

"I'm not interested in *that!*"

"There's no doubt he killed Larry, too."

"That's what I mean. Exactly! What are we going to do about it?"

"What do you mean?"

"You know *exactly* what I mean, damn it. I was just talking to the senator on the phone. He's flying in first thing in the morning. And keep *that* under your hat. Normally he wouldn't come here at a time like this. But he wants to know exactly where we stand. So I want you to give me the answers. *All* of them. Then we'll figure how this can best be handled."

Sumner licked his lips and shuffled his feet uncomfortably.

"Sit down, Conrad, for God's sake. I want to know *everything.* I want to know *exactly* what that sonofabitch Powell has to use against us."

"Actually, Hector, I really believe Powell wants to cooperate."

Prentice glared at him. "You think he'd miss a chance like this? Bah! Not on your life."

"I really think we should approach him, Hector."

Prentice made a brushing motion with his hand as if to push the idea away from him.

"Really, Hector, without his cooperation—"

"No! He'd play us for fools. Then when we lowered our guard —boom! He'd give it to us good."

Sumner rubbed his forehead painfully. "I just don't see how we can ... Larry was seen picking up Barbara Hancock in Bristow the night he was killed. Beatrix wrote Larry a note arranging to meet him and has no alibi for that night. Kit

Belman was supposed to be at a Unit School convention in Seattle the night of the murder, but Powell checked and Kit wasn't there. . . . And God knows what else Powell has up his sleeve. . . . All he has to do is leak these facts out to one of the senator's opposition newspapers and . . ."

"Are you saying Larry had *both* those women up there in his cottage?"

"I know it sounds incredible."

"My son never pretended to be a saint."

"But Beatrix. It's unbelievable. . . ."

"She was frigid. I got that from Corrine, my daughter. . . . Yes, I can see it. A frigid woman might try a stunt like that to see if it would stimulate— So what happened then?"

"Well, Kit pretended to be at the convention, followed Larry and Beatrix up to the cottage, caught them in the act and killed Larry. The Hancock woman was obviously in another room at the time, saw it and tried to blackmail Kit. So he killed her."

Prentice groaned like a wounded animal.

"So you see, Hector, it will be virtually impossible for us to conceal these facts. They're too closely interrelated to Barbara Hancock's death. Unless . . ."

"Unless what?"

"Unless Powell has got something up his sleeve that we don't know about. I keep thinking of what he said about this working out better than you think. I really feel it was his way of letting us know he was open to a deal."

"What's he want?"

"Justine Marshal has resigned. He obviously wants to be named temporary sheriff until the next election, at which time there's no doubt that he'll be elected. We have nobody on the slate who would stand a chance against him.

"Second, he'll want us to let up on the pressure to demote the authority of the sheriff's office. No state police in the valley, Hector."

Prentice was grim. "And just how much can he promise for all this?"

"That's something I don't know. I've about given up trying to second-guess him. But I have a strong feeling he has something up his sleeve."

"The thoughts of that guy sitting in the sheriff's office makes me sick."

"It might not be all that bad, Hector. No, please let me say this. Powell has no partisan politics. He isn't like Sandy Marshal in that respect. Personally, I think all he wants is to be left alone to run the sheriff's office. And, personally, I'd like to leave him alone and put my mind to other things—if you know what I mean."

Prentice wasn't a man to give ground easily. But in his fight for top spot he had learned something of give and take. "So what do you suggest?"

"Well—that we make the first overture, offer our friendship. He'll know why we're doing it. But that's as it has to be. It'll be up to him to take the initiative from there. At least we'll know where we stand."

"All right," Prentice said. "Let's go and talk to the sonofabitch."

11

Sam was alone in his office when the knock sounded at the door.

He reached into the drawer and snapped the tape machine onto *record.* Placing the parabolic microphone on the desk, he said, "Come in."

Sumner and Hector Prentice entered the office. Sumner closed the door. They both stood in front of Sam's desk.

"I won't beat around the bush," Prentice said, a little too loudly. "We know that the sheriff has resigned. We've both decided it would be best for the valley, for everybody concerned, if you were appointed temporary sheriff until the next election. Sumner and I are going to the county commissioners with that recommendation. I don't think there's any doubt that you will be appointed."

Sam smiled. "Well, that sure isn't what you'd call beating around the bush, all right. And I appreciate it, Hector. And I'll do everything I can for the valley."

"We're sure you will."

"Sam," Sumner said, "we heard about Kit Belman. Was it suicide?"

"Looks like it."

"What's going to become of all this mess, Sam? This scandal?"

"It's going to be a scandal, all right."

"Isn't there something we can do, some way we can—well, control it a little? You know."

"I don't see how we can, Connie. There's got to be a hearing and there's going to be a lot of interested people looking in. If we tried to hide something we'd all get ourselves in a lot of trouble. No. We've got to bring out all the facts."

"But, goddamn it!" Prentice exploded. "Damn it—"

"Easy, Hector," Sumner cut in quickly. "Let Sam have his say. Sam's right. . . . How do you see it, Sam?"

"Well," Sam said, "first of all, there's no sense in causing *unnecessary* scandal. So we decide what's important and what isn't important. So—first of all, there's that note we found in Larry's pocket. We forget about that note. That note isn't important."

Both Prentice and Sumner stared at him bug-eyed. A smile began playing at the corner of Sumner's lips as he glanced knowingly at Prentice.

Sam gazed thoughtfully off into space.

"Maybe Trixie and Larry had met each other for a drink at some time. I don't know. I don't care. It's nobody's business, because it had nothing to do with Larry's death. The fact is we have checked every lounge in the valley and in Bristow and Larry did not meet Trixie or any other woman at five-thirty on the day he was killed. Or on any other day, so near as we can find out. So the note has no bearing on his death. Right?"

"Right!" they said. "Right."

"Now, the state police talked with a drive-in attendant named Horace Johnson who saw Barbara Hancock get into a car in Bristow the night Larry was killed. He told the state police he thought it was a Lincoln. Anyway, I gave him a call and asked him if he'd be willing to state on a stack of Bibles in a courtroom it was a Lincoln, and he said that he couldn't really be that sure. I asked him if maybe it was a Mercury, and he said that, yes, the backs of them look quite a bit alike and maybe it could have been a '70 Mercury. So I had one of the deputies go up there and get a signed statement from him. He said he'd like it better that way, so that he wouldn't have to appear at the hearing."

Prentice and Sumner leaned toward him expectantly, their eyes glistening.

"We all know," Sam said, "that Kit Belman drives a '70 Mercury. Right?"

"Right!"

"So here's one way of looking at it. Everybody figured that Larry had left town on business. But we all know that sometimes he went up to his cottage just to be alone and think things out and do some fishing. Isn't that right, Hector?"

"Yes. Yes. That's absolutely right."

"So that's what he did. He hiked on up to his cottage to do some thinking and fishing. But Kit didn't know this. Kit had been up there on occasions with Larry to play cards and things, and I guess he knew where Larry kept the key hidden. So he arranged to meet Barbara at Bristow, then took her to Larry's cottage. He started in seducing her, and Larry came back from the creek where he had been doing some night fishing and found them. Kit panicked and they got in a fight and Kit killed him. Barbara ran away and Kit couldn't find her. Later she came to town and tried to blackmail him and he killed her." Sam looked at them. " 'Course there's no evidence left to prove any of this. But, looking at it from this particular angle, that explains it about as good as any. Wouldn't you say?"

"Perfect," Prentice exclaimed. "Perfect."

"Is that about the way you're going to present it at the hearing, Connie?"

Sumner could hardly contain himself. "Yes. We're going to have to bring all those facts out, all right. Yes. That's how we'll present it."

"You're to be congratulated on having solved this so quickly and—and—thoroughly," Prentice said.

"You've done an excellent job, Sam," Sumner said, offering his hand.

"I'm doing my job," Sam said, "the way I see it."

When they left he turned off the tape machine and phoned Doc Blainsworth. "Doc—about that semen you found on Larry's balls and his crotch hairs? You didn't put it on your report. Well, I think we can wrap this thing up pretty tidy if we just forget all about that part of it. It's just going to make things tough on Larry's wife and his family if we bring it out. And some of those out-of-town newspapers are going to grab it and make a political thing out of it against the senator, and that isn't going to do the valley one damn bit of good. So what do you say?"

"Why the hell d'you think I left it off in the first place?"

"Thanks, Doc."

He hung up and phoned Justine, who was at home with her mother. He asked her to come down to the office. She arrived within fifteen minutes.

"Sit down," he said. "Listen to this."

He played back the conversation among himself, Prentice and Sumner. She listened in silence. When the tape was finished he said, "And that's the way it ends. Nothing will be gained by *anybody* by your bringing out that confession of Wilbur's. I want that confession and I want the tape of your interview with him."

She nodded without argument, but her face was a picture of puzzlement. "I . . . I don't understand. Didn't . . . Wilbur kill Larry after all?"

"Sure he did."

"But—?"

"Let's go and get something to eat. I'll explain it to you."

12

They had finished the steaks and were enjoying the red wine.

"You see, Justine," Sam said, "under it all, Sumner and Prentice really believe that Larry Prentice was servicing two women the night he was killed—both Trixie and Barbara. But that isn't true."

She was very puzzled.

"Barbara was actually *being* serviced by Prentice *and* Kit Belman."

"My God!"

"When Wilbur killed Prentice, Belman was probably in another room."

"How did you realize this?"

"As soon as you played me Wilbur's confession."

"I don't understand."

"Wilbur said he found Prentice's clothes *on the chair beside the bed.* If Prentice had been wearing those clothes, his wallet would have been in them. But Pepe Poirier went into Prentice's cottage the next day and found Prentice's wallet in a suit in the closet."

"I see," she said. "Then you knew Wilbur had dressed Larry in somebody else's clothes."

"That's right."

"And because the wallet was also missing from the suit Prentice was wearing in the wrecked car, you knew whose suit it was, because Kit Belman was the only person who had opportunity to remove the wallet."

"Right. Then it all added up. Kit Belman and his wife located Larry's wrecked car. Kit planned to strip the suit off Larry's body while his wife was away phoning you—that way there'd be no car parked up on the road. But Henry Pike came along, and all Kit had time to do was get the wallet out of the suit—his own wallet.

"That's why he broke in here last night. To get the suit. Our investigations would have eventually shown it wasn't Larry's suit."

"And that's how you knew Trixie Belman had written the note."

"Sure."

"The note, then, was merely a note Trixie had written her husband."

"That's right."

"So the note really *didn't* have anything to do with the murder."

"Nothing at all."

She gazed at him in wonder. "Sam, why did you do it? Was it to stop the scandal?"

"You might say. The way I look at it, everybody responsible is dead. Let Hector think we did it to keep the Prentice name out of scandal. That won't hurt anybody. But the way I look at it, with Wilbur dead, nothing could be gained by proving he killed Prentice. And the little fellow—Bobby—he'd have to carry the weight of that around with him the rest of his life. There's no justice in that, Justine.

"Anyway, I'm not sure that if Wilbur had lived and stood trial, a jury selected from this valley would have found him guilty. It's an old unwritten law that if a man finds his wife being seduced by another man and he kills the other man while they are *flagrante delicto,* then it's justifiable homicide. True, he had separated them before he killed Prentice. But that's only a technicality of law. How do you think a valley jury would have judged him?"

"I don't know. But the thought has come to me—although I know it never entered your mind for a minute—that if Wilbur's part in this had been brought out, I would be down there in the old jailhouse—in jail—right now."

"Gee," he said with a grin and a great show of innocence. "I never thought of that."

Her eyes were moist with emotion. "You know, Sam, Dad once told Mother and me that you were—I think his words were 'the smartest young'—if you'll pardon the expression—'son of a bitch' that he ever worked with. I see now what he meant.

"And," she added, "it's very clear to me who belongs in that sheriff's chair."

13

Sam wasn't quite finished.

He drove his car, with Justine beside him, down a dark street and parked about half a block from the brightly lighted KTIT Radio and TV Building. (Kleinfeld's station wagon was parked in front.) He glanced at his watch, switched off the headlights and turned to Justine.

"This won't take long."

"I *beg* your pardon!"

"I said—"

"I heard what you said and I don't like it at all. I don't like—"

"But—"

"—the inference that you can merely pull over to some curb on a side street and that I would— Well, damn it, I won't, Sam. And I'm insulted that you should think I would."

"But—"

"And furthermore, I have *never* given you any reason to *ever* believe that it won't take long. I dislike the inference that I can be treated like a bloody rabbit. And I'm humiliated that you should attempt to treat me like some lakeside slut."

"But, Justine, you've got me wrong on this. I didn't mean it that way at all. You see, I've got a plan worked out—"

He was interrupted by Silvers's voice blasting through the two-way. "Car Powell! Car Powell! Home calling car Powell."

"Car Powell. Shoot."

"Sam, we've just had a report that Schuyler Kleinfeld's house is on fire. There's something wrong with the phone lines here. I can't ring out. Use your phone and call the fire department."

"No. I think we'll let the damned thing burn down. He's been a pain in the ass to us."

"That's a real good idea. He's got it coming to him."

Sam hung up the microphone and sat back.

"Sam!" Justine exclaimed. "You can't be serious?"

"You watch the front of the TV building."

And sure enough, in a matter of seconds Kleinfeld came charging out, stumbled and fell flat on the sidewalk, got up, leaped into his wagon and roared away.

"The bugger's got a radio up there all right," Sam said.

"Sam! You had this all planned."

He nodded. "He's beamed in on our frequency. That's how he kept on top of us all the time. Well, my new friend Hector

Prentice is buying that station. I'm going to use a little influence and get that radio jerked out of there."

"But you can't do that, Sam. Heavens, in Los Angeles every radio and TV station is beamed in on the police frequency."

"This isn't Los Angeles. KTIT has no opposition. We'll give them the news stories when we're ready to give them. It's the way it's always been. It's the way it's going to stay."

"You sound just like my dad."

He made no reply, and the startling thought came to her that perhaps he no longer wished to be compared with Sandy Marshal, that perhaps he wanted to—as they said in the valley—begin casting a shadow of his own.

He started the car and made a U-turn on the street.

"Where are we going, Sam?"

"I thought we might take a cruise up Bristow way."

She was silent until they had turned the corner and were approaching the four-laner, then, "Will it take long, do you think?"

"Yes," he said. "I think it'll take quite a while."

She snuggled close to him and felt very secure. He might not be Sandy Marshal. But he was sure as hell Sam Powell. And that put him second place to nobody.